**He'd Al
When It Came To Redheads
And Ladies In Distress. And
Brenna Montgomery Was Both—
All Wrapped Up Into One
Neat Little Package.**

He didn't doubt for a minute that the incident with Pete had scared her. Her pale complexion and the tremor in her voice had been quite genuine.

But he'd dealt with Brenna Montgomery's brand of trouble before and wanted no part of it. Her kind moved in and started trying to change everything in sight. Her complaint was proof enough of that. She hadn't even been a resident of Tranquillity two full weeks, and she was already trying to stop his uncle Pete's friendly tradition of welcoming newcomers to town by kissing them on the cheek.

Dylan shook his head. No doubt about it. That little lady was going to be trouble with a great, big capital *T*. Unfortunately, Brenna Montgomery had to be the best-looking trouble he'd ever laid eyes on....

Dear Reader,

Wondering what to put on your holiday wish list? How about six passionate, powerful and provocative new love stories from Silhouette Desire!

This month, bestselling author Barbara Boswell returns to Desire with our MAN OF THE MONTH, SD #1471, *All in the Game*, featuring a TV reality-show contestant who rekindles an off-screen romance with the chief cameraman while her identical twin wonders what's going on.

In SD #1472, *Expecting…and In Danger* by Eileen Wilks, a Connelly hero tries to protect and win the trust of a secretive, pregnant lover. It's the latest episode in the DYNASTIES: THE CONNELLYS series—the saga of a wealthy Chicago-based clan.

A desert prince loses his heart to a feisty intern in SD #1473, *Delaney's Desert Sheikh* by award-winning author Brenda Jackson. This title marks Jackson's debut as a Desire author. In SD #1474, *Taming the Prince* by Elizabeth Bevarly, a blue-collar bachelor trades his hard hat for a crown…and a wedding ring? This is the second Desire installment in the exciting CROWN AND GLORY series.

Matchmaking relatives unite an unlikely couple in SD #1475, *A Lawman in Her Stocking* by Kathie DeNosky. And SD #1476, *Do You Take This Enemy?* by reader favorite Sara Orwig, is a marriage-of-convenience story featuring a pregnant heroine whose groom is from a feuding family. This title is the first in Orwig's compelling STALLION PASS miniseries.

Make sure you get all six of Silhouette Desire's hot November romances.

Enjoy!

Joan Marlow Golan

Joan Marlow Golan
Senior Editor, Silhouette Desire

Please address questions and book requests to:
Silhouette Reader Service
U.S.: 3010 Walden Ave., P.O. Box 1325, Buffalo, NY 14269
Canadian: P.O. Box 609, Fort Erie, Ont. L2A 5X3

A Lawman in
Her Stocking
KATHIE DeNOSKY

Published by Silhouette Books
America's Publisher of Contemporary Romance

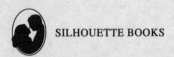

SILHOUETTE BOOKS

ISBN 0-373-76475-8

A LAWMAN IN HER STOCKING

Copyright © 2002 by Kathie DeNosky

This edition published by arrangement with Harlequin Books S.A.

® and TM are trademarks of Harlequin Books S.A., used under license.
Trademarks indicated with ® are registered in the United States Patent
and Trademark Office, the Canadian Trade Marks Office and in other
countries.

Visit Silhouette at www.eHarlequin.com

Printed in U.S.A.

KATHIE DeNOSKY

lives in her native southern Illinois with her husband, three children and two very spoiled dogs. She writes highly sensual stories with a generous amount of humor. Kathie's books have appeared on the Waldenbooks bestseller list. She enjoys going to rodeos, traveling to research settings for her books and listening to country music. She often starts her day at 2:00 a.m., so she can write without interruption, before the rest of the family is up and about. You may write to Kathie at P.O. Box 2064, Herrin, IL 62948-5264 or e-mail her at kathie@kathiedenosky.com.

To Rox, Belinda and Ginny.
Thanks for sharing the laughter and fun. Love you guys.

One

"Sheriff? Are you in here?"

At the sound of the female voice echoing through the cavernous firehouse side of Tranquillity's Sheriff's Office and Fire Department, Dylan Chandler's stomach twisted into a tight knot and the hair on the back of his neck stood straight up. He hated when a woman used that tone—fear tinged with indignation. In all his years as an officer of the law, he'd never seen it fail to be the prelude to big trouble.

He gripped the rafter with his gloved hand to steady himself, glanced down over his bare shoulder and stifled a groan. He'd been right in his assessment. Tranquillity's newest resident, Brenna Montgomery, looked like she'd seen a ghost, and it appeared that she'd been thoroughly pissed off by the encounter, too.

Dylan had only seen her once before, and that had been from a distance. He'd arrived late the night she'd shown up at the town council meeting to apply for a permit to open her craft shop, so they hadn't been formally introduced. And if her expression held any clue to the nature of her visit now, he didn't think he'd be able to work up much enthusiasm for getting acquainted.

Maybe if he remained silent, she wouldn't notice him dangling from a rope high above her head and wander back into the adjoining sheriff's office. At least long enough for him to climb down and put on his shirt.

But sure as shootin', she spotted the end of the rope dangling close to the wall, her gaze following it to his less than dignified position among the rafters of the firehouse. He groaned. Nothing left to do now but introduce himself.

"I'm Sheriff Chandler. What can I do for you, ma'am?"

He braced his feet against the wall, rappelled down to where she stood, and grabbed his shirt. Shrugging into it, he jammed the tail into his jeans as he waited for her to say something.

When she remained silent and continued to stare at him, he decided she probably thought he was some kind of a nut. Either that, or his fly was open. He made a show of glancing at his boots. His zipper was closed, but he still wore the climbing harness around his waist and upper thighs. Snug as it was, the webbed straps pulled his jeans tight and brought the male parts of his anatomy into stark relief.

"What did you need, Ms. Montgomery?" he

prompted as he hastily removed the nylon straps and tossed them on the chair where his shirt had been.

The dazed look in her pretty blue eyes suddenly cleared and her cheeks colored a rosy pink. Averting her astonished gaze to the rafters, she asked, ''Why on earth were you hanging from the ceiling?''

Hot damn! She'd been checking him out.

In an effort to hide the grin pulling at the corners of his mouth, he used the cuff of his sleeve to buff a spot of imaginary dust from the silver star pinned to his chambray shirt. ''I had to test some new climbing equipment for the Search and Rescue Team.''

She nodded, but kept silent as she glanced around the firehouse. He almost laughed out loud. It seemed the lady was having trouble looking him in the eye.

After several moments of awkward silence, Dylan placed his hand at her lower back and guided her through the door into the adjoining sheriff's office. Walking behind the desk, he flexed his hand in an effort to stop the tingling that ran the length of his arm and spread throughout his torso. He'd probably been gripping the rope too tight, he decided. It was just plain ridiculous to think it had anything to do with feeling the warmth of her skin through the crisp fabric of her blouse.

''Now, why don't you tell me what's bothering you, Ms. Montgomery?'' he suggested, removing his wide-brimmed Resistol from a hook on the wall. He jammed it onto his head before turning to face her.

While he waited for her to collect her thoughts, his gaze traveled to her copper-colored hair. For the life of him, he couldn't figure out why she'd piled it on top of her head in that god-awful knot. It looked like a baseball plopped down in the middle of a bird's nest.

"I want to report an elderly gentleman—" She stopped abruptly. "Sheriff, are you listening to me?"

She'd planted her fists on her shapely hips, drawing his attention to her feminine form. She expected him to listen with a distraction like that?

"Now what was that about an old man?" he managed to ask.

"I said there's an elderly gentleman accosting women on Main Street."

"Here? In Tranquillity? Are you sure?"

Dylan watched her cheeks flush with indignation at his dubious questions. The color highlighted the few golden freckles sprinkled across the bridge of her nose. Her big blue eyes and perfectly shaped lips made him think of long winter nights snuggled beneath the covers of his king-size bed.

He shook his head to dislodge the wayward thought. She'd said something else, but he'd missed it again. *Damn!* He'd better get his mind off the woman's looks and back to the business at hand.

"What was that?"

"I told you the old guy just grabbed me and kissed me," she stated, her patience clearly wearing thinner by the minute.

Dylan heaved a sigh as he looked over the top of her head to stare out the plate-glass window of his orderly office. What had happened to the pleasant lady who charmed the socks off the all-male town council? All the mayor and town council members had been able to talk about for the past week was what a sweet little gal that Montgomery woman was.

He shook his head. It never ceased to amaze him how a female could be so amiable when things went her way and how quarrelsome she could get when they didn't.

Turning his attention back to the woman standing on the other side of the desk, he silently cursed. He could deal with her insistence and tone of voice easy enough. It was the way she looked that made sweat pop out on his forehead and upper lip. Why did Brenna Montgomery have to be so darned…cute?

But what was up with her clothes? he wondered when her long skirt rustled. Her white, ruffled collar went clear up to her chin and her black skirt just barely cleared the floor. Dressed as she was, she reminded him of the schoolmarms in the old, western movies he'd watched as a kid.

"That's all there was to it?" he finally asked. "Just a simple kiss?"

"Wasn't that enough?" When he remained silent, she looked incredulous. "Surely you don't think I'd make up something like this?"

"No."

His stomach did a back flip. It didn't matter how her hair was styled, what kind of clothes she wore, or how kissable her lips looked; he'd always been a sucker when it came to redheads and ladies in distress. And Brenna Montgomery was both—all wrapped up into one neat little package.

Brenna felt a shiver slither up her spine and her tendency to crave chocolate whenever she became nervous rushed forward as the sheriff's brilliant, green gaze narrowed on her upturned face. She'd been so shocked to find the man shirtless and dangling from the firehouse ceiling, she hadn't noticed anything about him beyond his various muscle groups.

And what impressive, well-defined muscle groups they were, too. Bulging biceps, a ridged stomach and all that masculine bare skin had taken her by surprise. But the sight of the webbed harness pulling the denim tight across his impressive attributes had struck her absolutely speechless.

Sheriff Dylan Chandler certainly wasn't the average, run-of-the-mill, civil servant. In fact, she couldn't find one darned thing average or ordinary about the man.

His badge certified he was supposed to be one of the good guys. But didn't they wear white hats? His cowboy hat was outlaw-black, and combined with the lock of ebony hair hanging low on his forehead and the five o'clock shadow covering his lean cheeks, he appeared a little wild, relatively dangerous and totally fascinating.

Irritated with herself for giving the man's rugged good looks and bulging muscle mass a second thought, she took a deep breath, shored up her courage and asked, "What do you intend to do about this?"

Dylan pushed back the brim of his Resistol with his thumb, then folded his arms across his chest. He'd stopped several barroom bawls before they ever got started with that narrow-eyed stare he'd just given her. And for a second or two, he'd thought she might back down. But it was clear she wasn't intimidated by him. Nope. Not even a little bit.

He almost smiled. For the first time in six years,

his bluff had been called. And by a cute little redhead with freckles, no less. Amazing!

"Do you want to file a formal complaint, Ms. Montgomery?"

When she carefully avoided his gaze, he decided that he might not be losing his touch after all.

"No, I'm not going to file a complaint," she said, brushing imaginary lint from her skirt. "The old guy didn't exactly threaten me." She squared her shoulders and finally met his gaze head-on. "But I don't want it to happen again. I found it very frightening to have a total stranger grab me in a bear hug and kiss me. Even if it was on the cheek."

"I understand, Ms. Montgomery. Did the old gent hand you a rose just before he kissed you?" When she nodded, Dylan grinned. "I have a good idea who you're talking about, and believe me, you were in no danger. I'll ask him about it, but it's my bet you've just been officially welcomed to town by Pete Winstead."

"I don't care who he is," she said. "The man scared the bejeebers out of me."

Dylan frowned. "It was only a little peck on the cheek."

"Yes, but you have no idea how frightening something like that can be for a woman." She seemed to be gathering a full head of steam as she stared at him, and the heightening color on her pale cheeks fascinated the hell out of him. "Where I come from, his actions might even be considered an…" She paused as if searching for the right word, then glaring at him, finished, "…an assault."

Dylan couldn't help himself. He laughed out loud.

"Did the old geezer say anything during this alleged *assault?*"

The glare she sent his way was so heated it could have fried bacon. "Yes, but I was so frightened, I didn't understand what he said." She wrinkled her cute little nose. "Besides, he smelled like beer."

Dylan's grin instantly disappeared. "You have something against a man drinking a beer after a hard day's work?"

"Well…no—"

"Then let me clue you in on the way things are around these parts, Ms. Montgomery. Nearly every man in town stops by Luke's Bar and Grill after work for a beer and the latest gossip. It's a tradition—drink a beer, swap a story or two and go home." Dylan shrugged. "Pete's no different than the rest of us. He goes to Luke's regularly. But I've never known him to drink more than two beers at one sitting."

"I realize this is a tight-knit, little community and, believe me, I want to be a part of it just like everyone else." Her ankle-length skirt rustled like a bed of dry leaves when she tapped her toe. "But Pete Winstead's drinking habits aren't the issue here. When a stranger grabs a woman and kisses her, it can be very frightening. It's your job to prevent things like that from happening."

Dylan's arms dropped to his sides, his hands flexing in frustration. He was good at his job and he didn't need a high-strung, big-city female telling him how to do it. He'd had that happen once, he wasn't going to allow it to happen a second time.

He leaned forward and braced his hands on the polished surface of the desk. "I said I'd talk to him.

Now, is there anything else you feel the need to complain about, Ms. Montgomery?''

"It wouldn't do me any good if I did, now would it, Sheriff?'' She'd managed to make his title sound like a dirty word.

Before he had a chance to respond, she turned on her heel and slammed the door behind her so hard that the plate-glass window rattled ominously.

Shoving his hands in the front pockets of his jeans, Dylan silently watched her march across the street, gather the yards of her ridiculous skirt into a bunch around her knees and stuff it all into an aging Toyota.

He didn't doubt for a minute that the incident with Pete had scared the hell out of her. Her pale complexion and the tremor in her voice when she walked into the firehouse had been quite genuine.

But he'd dealt with Brenna Montgomery's brand of trouble before and wanted no part of it. Her kind moved in and started trying to change everything in sight. Her complaint was proof enough of that. She hadn't even been a resident of Tranquillity two full weeks and she was already trying to stop his uncle Pete's friendly tradition.

Dylan shook his head. No doubt about it. That little lady was going to be trouble with a great big, capital *T*. Unfortunately, even in those weird clothes Brenna Montgomery had to be the best-looking trouble he'd ever laid eyes on.

And he had a feeling if she stayed in town, Tranquillity would never be the same.

"Get a grip, Brenna. The sheriff's probably right about old Deke,'' Abigail Montgomery said.

"Pete," Brenna corrected her grandmother. "The old man's name is Pete."

Abigail waved her hand dismissively. "Whatever. I'm not interested in the old goat. I want to know more about the hunk wearing the badge."

Brenna sighed. She and her grandmother had been down this road before. "What's to tell? He listened to my complaint, then gave me his biased opinion."

Abigail's bright orange curls danced as she shook her head. "You know what I mean. What color are his eyes and hair? How tall is he? Is he a super stud or a major dud?"

Exasperated, Brenna stared at the woman. Since her retirement a little over a year ago as a high school guidance counselor, Abigail had made it her sole purpose in life to find Brenna a husband. She'd even gone so far as to sell the house she and Brenna had shared since the death of Brenna's parents ten years ago to move to Tranquillity, Texas, with Brenna in order to keep up the pressure.

"Granny, every time I meet a man, we go through this same inquisition. Aren't you getting a little tired of it?"

"Brenna Elaine Montgomery, you're almost twenty-six years old and the only thing you've had that even resembles a serious relationship was a college fling with that jerk, Tim Miller."

"Tom Mitchell," Brenna said, making a face. "And he taught me a valuable lesson—men use women, then cast them aside when they're done."

"If you'll remember, I told you from the beginning he reminded me of a weasel. And when he talked you into helping him get through law school, I knew I was right.'' Abigail shook her head. ''But don't judge all men by that loser.''

Brenna felt her cheeks heat with embarrassment. ''Well, I haven't seen a man yet who could tempt me into finding out if my first assessment was wrong.''

Abigail gave her a knowing look. ''Maybe old Devin—''

''Dylan.''

''Whatever. Maybe he'll prove you wrong.'' Her grandmother's gray eyes twinkled merrily. ''You know, that's probably why you're so uptight all the time. You need a man like Darwin in your life and a little hanky-panky to help you unwind.''

''Granny!''

''I just call it the way I see it.'' Abigail pushed the sleeves of her hot-pink, nylon warm-up jacket to her elbows and leaned forward in the ladder-back chair. ''Now, tell me about Sheriff Chancellor. You know I never get tired of talking about good-looking men.''

''His name is Chandler.''

''Whatever.''

Brenna frowned. ''You're not going to let this go, are you?''

''Absolutely not.'' Abigail winked. ''I'll bet my new Reeboks this guy is a real stud. Probably better-looking than Mel Gibson and muscled up like Ronald Schwasenhoofer.''

''Arnold Schwarzenegger.''

''Whatever.''

Brenna rose from the table to place her plate in the dishwasher. She was only delaying the inevitable. Abigail Montgomery could have been a top-notch interrogator for the CIA.

"Just how did you arrive at your conclusion that the sheriff had to be something special?"

"I didn't deal with teenagers for over forty years and not learn to recognize a hedge job when I see one," Abigail shot back. "You think he's a hunk."

"I do not."

"Do too. Now spill it."

Brenna threw up her hands, as much in exasperation as in surrender. "He's tall—"

"How tall?" Abigail pressed.

"I'd say he's a little over six feet tall and has black hair and green eyes." When her grandmother frowned at the lack of information, Brenna tried to sound indifferent. "He looks to be somewhere in his early thirties. Now, that's all I know about the man. And all I care to know."

"Uh-oh! He must have a spare tire around his waist." Abigail shook her head. "Don't worry. The way you cook, the extra weight will drop off the poor man like leaves from a tree."

Brenna ignored the remark about her lack of cooking skills as she remembered the sheriff's assortment of lean muscles. Her mouth went dry. "His stomach is actually quite flat."

"No teeth?"

A picture of his devastating smile flitted through Brenna's mind. "He has beautiful teeth."

"Got a real honker, huh?"

"Granny, will you stop?" Brenna placed her hands on her hips as she fought back a smile. "He doesn't have a big nose. And even if he did, I doubt that it would detract from his good looks."

"Ah-ha!" Abigail cried triumphantly. "Now we're

getting down to the nitty gritty. He's *that* good-looking, huh?" She gave Brenna a wink and a wicked grin. "I'll bet he's a hell of a kisser, too."

"Granny—"

"Are you going to need the car tonight?" Abigail asked, suddenly.

Dazed at how fast her grandmother had changed subjects, Brenna shook her head. "No, I can walk to class. Why?"

"I wanted to drive down to Alpine with one of my new friends."

"That will be nice," Brenna said, glad her grandmother had made friends so soon after their move to Tranquillity. "What do you have planned?"

Abigail's grin turned wicked. "We're going cruising for a stud muffin for you. Any preferences?"

"Granny, please don't start in again with the you-need-a-husband routine."

"Oh, lighten up," Abigail said, rolling her eyes. "We're just going to a movie. Want me to drop you off at the town hall?"

Brenna breathed a sigh of relief. She was never quite sure when the woman was serious and when she wasn't. "No, thanks. It's not far, and I need the exercise."

Her grandmother shook her head. "I can't figure out why you're so concerned about staying in shape if you aren't interested in attracting a man."

"Granny—"

"Okay. I'll shut up for now," Abigail said, glancing at her Mickey Mouse watch. "Time to pick up my friend." She propelled herself from the chair and started into the living room. Turning back she shook her finger at Brenna. "Just remember I'd like to have a great-grandchild before I'm too senile to appreciate it. And that Sheriff Antler—"

"Chandler."

"Whatever," Abigail said, waving her hand. "He sounds like a great prospect for the father."

With that parting shot, Abigail breezed from the room in a flurry of hot-pink nylon and orange curls, leaving Brenna to wonder what sort of ridiculous fantasies her grandmother would start weaving about the town's insufferable sheriff.

Enjoying the mild, southwest Texas weather as she walked the short distance to the center of town, Brenna admired the rugged Davis Mountains a few miles away. Draped in the purpled shadows of early evening, the view was breathtaking and she forgot all about Abigail's matchmaking attempts as she focused on the nervous anticipation filling every cell in her body.

She took a deep breath to help settle the butterflies in her stomach and tamped down the need for something chocolate. She was going to do this. She was going to dig down deep inside and find the courage to share her love of handmade crafts with the women of Tranquillity. It was a big part of her plan to reinvent herself and she wasn't going to wimp out now. Besides, Tom had told her several times in the course of their four-year relationship that her dream of starting her own business and teaching Folk Art was silly and unprofitable. Brenna clenched her teeth. She had come a long way in the year since Tom decided that he had more in common with a woman in his law class than he had with her. But she still had a few things left to accomplish. She had every intention of proving him wrong about her teaching Folk Art, as well as his prediction that she'd never break her habit of reaching for something chocolate whenever she became nervous or upset.

By the time she reached the community room in the town hall, more than two dozen women milled around the display she'd set up earlier in the day, while others had already found a place for themselves at the work tables. Thrilled by the number of people in attendance, Brenna smiled as she walked into the room. Her only regret was that Tom wasn't around so she could tell him how wrong he'd been.

"My dear, this is the best thing that's happened to Tranquillity in decades," Mrs. Worthington said, stepping forward. "I just know you'll help add culture to our little community. It's something I've sorely missed since I married Myron and moved from the East."

Brenna smiled. Cornelia Worthington was the mayor's wife, chairwoman of the Beautification Society and self-appointed matriarch of Tranquillity. Her approval could make or break Brenna's classes.

"Thank you, Mrs. Worthington," she said slowly, searching for the most tactful way to explain that Folk Art painting wasn't in the same category with Rembrandt or van Gogh. "But I'm afraid this class will fall short of the benefits you have in mind. It's considered more of a craft than fine art."

"Oh, what a dear," Mrs. Worthington said, turning to the ladies behind her. "She has such a modest attitude for someone so immensely talented. I'm so glad

I discovered her and persuaded her to instruct this class.''

Brenna barely managed to keep her mouth from dropping open. She practically had to beg the woman for the use of the room, since it was overseen by the Beautification Society.

''Ladies, if you'll please take your seats, we'll get started,'' she said, shaking her head and walking to the front of the room.

''Mildred, what took you so long?'' she heard Mrs. Worthington call to a late arrival.

''My car broke down on the way home from work,'' the woman said, sounding flustered. ''Fortunately, Dylan passed by on his way to the poker game over at Luke's and offered me a ride.''

''Dylan!'' Mrs. Worthington's voice turned to syrup. ''It's simply marvelous to see a man take an interest in the arts.''

At the mention of the sheriff's name, Brenna cringed and slowly turned around. Sure enough, there the man stood, leaning against the door frame, a self-assured smile plastered on his masculine lips. His confidence grated on her nerves and reminded her of their earlier confrontation.

But they were on her turf now. Things were going to be vastly different from the first time they'd met.

Dylan swallowed hard when he noticed Brenna moving toward him. He was having the devil of a time accepting the way she looked now, as opposed to earlier. If he'd thought she was cute then, in that hideous, old-fashioned get-up, he'd sadly underestimated her attractiveness.

He no longer had to wonder about the curves hidden by yards of fabric, or the length of her hair. Hell's bells, he almost wished he did. It would definitely be easier on him than the reality he faced now.

Her light blue shirt loosely caressed high, full breasts, while her faded jeans outlined nicely shaped legs and hips that swayed slightly as she walked. Her copper hair, shot with gold, brushed her waist and looked so soft, his fingers burned to thread themselves in the silken waves.

"Dylan, dear, you look a little feverish." Mildred patted his arm sympathetically. "Are you feeling all right?"

Hell no! He felt like he'd just been run down by a herd of stampeding longhorns. He had to swallow hard to get words to form in his suddenly dry mouth. "Uh…sure. I'm fine."

He quickly looked around to see if anyone else detected his discomfort. Noting several curious stares, Dylan cursed his luck.

The room boasted the largest collection of gossips he'd seen since arresting Jed Phelps for getting drunk and crashing Corny's Tupperware party. And that had been three years ago. If the old hens thought there was even a remote possibility that he found Brenna Montgomery attractive, they'd be like sharks in a feeding frenzy.

He glanced over at the woman standing beside him. Mildred Bruner was the county clerk and responsible for issuing all the marriage licenses in the county. It was common knowledge she was an incurable romantic and carried her book of forms everywhere she went just hoping someone would stop her and ask to apply for a ticket to wedded bliss.

He shifted from one foot to the other. If he didn't leave, and damned quick, Mildred would start digging around in that suitcase of a purse she carried, trying to find her license book, and by sunrise the rest of the busybodies would have everyone in town taking bets on when the wedding would take place. He silently ran through every curse word he knew. He wasn't looking for a wife, and even if he was, Brenna Montgomery wasn't likely to ever be a candidate.

"I'll be over at Luke's if you need a ride home, Mildred."

His cheeks burned as he watched several of the women smile knowingly. If they hadn't noticed he was having a problem before, they sure as hell would now. His voice hadn't sounded that uneven since puberty.

"You aren't staying for class, Sheriff?" Brenna asked when he headed for the door.

Dylan stopped dead in his tracks. He couldn't believe his ears. Brenna Montgomery wanted him in her painting class about as much as a poor, lost soul wanted to see a heat wave in hell.

He turned to face her, his scowl deepening. "No."

"That's a shame. Some of the most talented crafts-people I know are men."

She took a step in Dylan's direction. He took a step back. What was the woman up to now?

She thoughtfully tilted her head, her blue eyes dancing. "Of course, some men lack the patience and coordination it takes to learn the techniques."

Her challenge punched him right square in his ego.

When she took another step forward, Dylan stood his ground and reaching out, took her hand in his. "Oh, I'm sure I could master *any* technique, Ms. Montgomery. And I'm *very* patient."

The moment their fingers touched, a tingle raced the length of Dylan's arm, making his blood pressure skyrocket. But pride wouldn't allow him to back down. "I've never had any trouble getting my hands to do what I want," he assured. Letting a provocative drawl warm his words, he smiled suggestively. "Nor have I ever had anyone complain about their ability to obtain a satisfying result."

She jerked her hand out of his so fast, he thought she might have sprained her wrist.

"It was nice of you to stop by, Sheriff, but you'll have to excuse me. I need to start my class. I'm sure you can find your way out."

Dylan knew for sure he'd turned the tables. He could tell Brenna had been as affected by the touch of his hand as he'd been by hers. And, she was trying to give him the bum's rush.

But he'd be damned before he let it happen. She'd started this confrontation. He intended to finish it.

"Where do you want me to sit?"

Her eyes grew round. "You...you don't mean you're staying?"

"Yep." At her stunned reaction, he didn't even try to hold back his satisfied smile. "That's exactly what I mean."

"Oh, this is wonderful," old Corny said, clapping her pudgy hands to gain the women's attention. "Now that Dylan's taking the class, we shouldn't have any trouble convincing our men they could use a measure of culture, too. I intend to speak with My-ron about it this very evening, and I encourage every one of you to do the same with your husbands.''

Dylan's triumphant grin evaporated, and he barely controlled the urge to squirm when several of the women bobbed their heads in eager agreement. He'd forgotten all about the guys over at Luke's. Once they got wind he was taking an art class, he'd never hear the end of it. Now, short of humiliating himself in front of the entire room full of world-class busybod-ies, there wasn't any way out.

Every Tuesday night for no telling how long, he'd miss the poker game over at Luke's. He'd be forced to listen to Brenna's soft voice as she instructed the class. He'd have to watch her silky, red hair brush the top of her shapely rear—

His body tightened noticeably, and muttering a curse, he removed his Resistol, lowered it to zipper level and took a seat. As he sat watching Brenna, his mood lightened and he fought back a grin. If any good came out of this mess, it had to be the dazed look on her face.

Brenna Montgomery looked like she'd just sat down on a bumblebee.

Two

Dazed, Brenna turned and slowly walked to the front of the class. What had she been thinking? The sheriff had been ready to leave. And he would have, if she'd just kept her mouth shut.

But, no. She couldn't leave well enough alone. She'd tried to get even for this afternoon's disagreement—tried to practice being assertive—and ended up making a mess of everything. Becoming a stronger, more self-assured woman was a balancing act. And she'd just proven she was tilting a little too far to one side.

"Okay, ladies…and gentleman." She purposely avoided looking at the man as she handed out the supply lists. "These are the items you'll need for the course."

"What's the difference between Folk Art and

painting a landscape or a portrait?'' one of the women asked.

Brenna perched on the edge of the desk as she tried to organize her tangled thoughts. The sheriff's presence was playing havoc with her already jangled nerves and had her ready to kill for a Hershey bar.

''Originally the label Folk Art was given to all forms of art created by people who knew little, if anything, about method or design. A folk artist 'created' without knowing how or what they'd done. Fine art requires more disciplined techniques.''

''How did it get started?'' Mildred Bruner asked.

''You could say it evolved out of envy,'' Brenna answered, trying her best to ignore the man sitting in the back of the room. He was grinning like the Cheshire cat. ''In Europe, peasants wanted to simulate the expensive furnishings of the noble class, so they used Folk Art to paint their furniture, dishes and pottery. They even used it on store signs.''

Mrs. Worthington frowned. ''Store signs?''

Brenna nodded. ''Around the seventeenth and eighteenth century, the craft was used for practical, as well as decorative, purposes. Most of the common people were illiterate. But by having signs painted with bright colors and bold designs, shopkeepers could effectively advertise their product.'' She paused as she searched for an example. ''Let's say Luke's had a wooden sign with nothing more than a large beer stein with suds running down the side.'' She smiled. ''I don't think any of us would be left to wonder what Luke sold, would we?''

''Oh, how quaint,'' Mrs. Worthington said, her face brightening with a wide smile.

By the time Brenna went over what the ladies and Sheriff Chandler could expect to learn, it was almost time to dismiss the class. "Are there any more questions?" When no one responded, she smiled. "Then I'll dismiss class early. I have all the supplies at my shop. Stop by and I'll help you find everything you need so we can start painting next week."

On their way out, several of the ladies stopped to tell Brenna how enthusiastic they were about the class and to inquire about her new craft shop. Her spirits soared and the incident with the sheriff was all but forgotten as she closed the door to the community room and stepped out into the late-November night.

She'd accomplished two very important goals tonight. She'd generated a lot of interest in her new business, but more important, she'd found the courage to stand in front of a class to teach. She only wished Tom had been around to see just how far she'd come in the year since he'd dumped her, and how wrong he'd been about her ambitions.

Thinking about the man who'd taken her to the cleaners, both emotionally and financially, she cringed. How could she have been so naive, so blind about his self-centeredness?

"Ms. Montgomery, could I have a word with you?" a male voice asked from behind her at the same time a hand came down on her shoulder.

Her surprised cry echoed through the deserted streets of Tranquillity as she spun around and swung her tote, her aim directed where it would hurt the most—her assailant's groin.

"Take it easy, lady," Dylan said, quickly turning his body to protect himself. "It's just me."

"Sheriff Chandler!" She placed her hand over her heart as she glared at him. "Do all the men in this town get some kind of kick out of frightening women?"

Dylan stepped closer and hooked his thumbs in his belt loops. He couldn't understand why she'd been so upset about the incident with Pete. If the way she swung that bag was any indication, she could easily take care of herself.

"I didn't mean to scare you," he said, thankful that he'd been quick enough to side-step her blow. If he hadn't, he'd be writhing around on the sidewalk right now, feeling as if death would be a blessing. "I was just trying to stay out of the way until I could talk to you in private."

"Do you want to withdraw from the class?" she asked, sounding hopeful.

Nothing would make him happier. But he'd be damned before he gave her the satisfaction. "Nope. I think I'm going to enjoy learning to paint," he lied.

Her hopeful smile vanished. "That's nice, Sheriff. Now, if you'll excuse me, I need to be going."

Dylan frowned. That was the second time this evening that she'd tried to dismiss him. And it didn't sit any better this time than it had the last.

"Not so fast, Ms. Montgomery. We need to talk about what happened this afternoon."

She shook her head as she stared up at him. "I really don't see the need, Sheriff. I told you what happened. And you made it quite clear that you thought I was overreacting to the situation."

Dylan studied her upturned face for several long seconds. She really was the best-looking trouble he'd seen in years. Her guileless blue eyes held an intelligence that he found sexy as hell and her perfect cupid's bow lips were just begging to be kissed.

The ridiculous thought caused his stomach to twist into a tight knot. Thinking along those lines could get a man in serious trouble. He'd been there once and he had no intention of ever going there again.

Taking a deep breath, he nodded in the direction of the restaurant across the street. "Let's talk this out over a cup of coffee."

"But aren't you supposed to give Mildred Bruner a ride home?" she asked, looking around.

"Corny...Mrs. Worthington, whisked Mildred away about ten minutes ago, along with the rest of the class." He chuckled and shook his head when he thought of the flurry of flowered polyester as the women crowded into Corny's pink Cadillac and Helen Washburn's old Buick. "They mentioned something about an emergency meeting of the B.S. Club."

Brenna arched a perfectly shaped brow. "B.S. Club?"

"Uh...Beautification Society."

Way to go, Chandler. He'd just slipped up and told her the men's secret name for the town's only women's organization. A name that the men knew better than to mention in front of any of the club's members.

He cleared his throat. "They...uh, get together once or twice a month and share the latest gossip."

"I get the distinct impression that secrets aren't kept for very long around here," she said.

"Everyone knowing your business is one of the

hazards of living in a small town," he said, relieved that she'd let his less than flattering reference to the organization pass. He placed a hand on her back to usher her across the quiet street and felt a jolt travel up his arm and spread across his chest.

"Just a minute, Sheriff," she said, stiffening beneath his touch. "Why can't we talk right here?"

A slight tremor coursed through her, and he knew it had nothing to do with the chill of the autumn evening.

Good. At least he wasn't the only one affected by the contact.

"I wouldn't be much of a gentleman if I asked you to stand out here in the night air." He did his best to suppress a knowing grin as he added, "You're already shivering."

He almost laughed out loud when he had to trot to keep up with her as she marched across the street to Luke's.

Brenna had only been in Luke's Bar and Grill twice in the two weeks she'd been in Tranquillity, but both times she felt as if she'd taken a step back in time. Wanted posters from the late 1800s decorated the walls, along with cow skulls, branding irons and various pieces of old, leather harness. Shiny, brass spittoons were placed on the floor at either end of the bar and the room's muted light filtered down from suspended wagon wheels with antique lanterns converted to accommodate electricity.

Sheriff Chandler must have noticed her curiosity as he led the way to an empty table on the far side of the room. "Luke's granddaddy opened the saloon around the turn of the century and Luke is pretty sentimental about the place.'' He held a chair for her. ''How do you take your coffee?''

''With cream.''

She watched his long-legged stride carry him to the bar. Sheriff Chandler was as good-looking from the back as he was from the front, she decided. He had the widest shoulders, longest legs and the tightest butt—

Stunned by the direction her thoughts had taken, Brenna quickly looked away. Had she lost her mind? She had absolutely no interest in Dylan Chandler. No way. None.

''Here you go,'' he said, returning with their coffee. He placed two mugs on the table, then seated himself in the chair opposite her.

Taking a sip of the steamy liquid, Brenna listened to a country ballad playing on the jukebox as she waited for him to tell her what was on his mind. She wanted to get this over and put some distance between them. Something about the man made her insides quiver and her nerves tingle. And she was mere seconds away from going in search of the nearest candy machine for a chocolate fix.

Unable to stand the tension any longer, she cleared her throat and asked, ''What was it you wanted to talk about, Sheriff?''

He smiled at her over the top of his cup, making her heart skip a beat. ''You got the wrong impression this afternoon and I'd like to set things straight.'' She started to interrupt, but he held up a hand. ''I wasn't making light of the situation. But this is a small town, with small-town ways. When someone moves in, most everyone tries to do the neighborly thing and welcome the newcomer with open arms.'' He chuckled. ''I'll admit most folks are a little more subtle than Pete, but believe me, he has the best intentions. After you left the office, I talked to him and it was just as I thought—he was only trying to make you feel a part of the community.''

Brenna set her cup down and tried to ignore the tingling sensation skimming up her spine from the sound of his smooth baritone. ''Before today, I'd never laid eyes on the man. How was I to know about his neighborly tradition?''

''I'm sure it was unnerving,'' he said, nodding. ''But that's not why I wanted to talk to you.''

''If that's not it, then what's the purpose of this?''

''I think you have the right to know why I was so defensive about Pete.''

''Okay, I'm listening, Sheriff. Why don't you explain it to me?''

''Will you stop that?'' For reasons he'd rather not dwell on, Dylan wanted to hear her velvet voice say his name. ''Call me Dylan.''

''Okay…*Dylan*. Why are you so protective of Pete?''

He slowly placed his cup on the table as he tried to collect his thoughts. Maybe it hadn't been such a good idea, insisting that she use his name. The sound had sent his blood pressure up a couple of dozen points and made his mouth go dry.

''If you'll remember, I told you I've known Pete all my life,'' he said, finally forcing words past the cotton in his throat. ''In fact, he lives with me.''

Dylan paused. This was the part he dreaded. But it

would be better coming from him than from someone else. And she'd find out soon enough anyway.

Clearing his throat, he met her expectant gaze head-on. "Pete Winstead is my uncle."

Her expressive blue eyes widened. "No wonder you were so adamant about him being harmless. Why didn't you tell me this afternoon?"

Relieved she wasn't throwing something at him for withholding that bit of information, Dylan grinned. "To tell the truth, I was pretty frustrated about the whole thing. I've warned him for years that something like this might happen." He shrugged. "Anyway, I think Pete will be a lot less enthusiastic about his greetings from now on. He was pretty upset that he'd frightened you and made me promise to talk to you the first chance I got."

"I can understand your frustration," she said, nodding. "I live with a pretty eccentric relative of my own. I hope Pete's not too upset."

Her lips turned up and Dylan felt as if he'd been kicked in the gut. Brenna Montgomery could drop a three hundred pound lumberjack with that smile of hers.

"Don't worry about Pete." Dylan cringed at the rust in his voice. Clearing his throat, he went on, "He'll get over it. Nothing gets him down for long."

"He sounds like my grandmother." Grinning, she shook her head. "On second thought, I don't think anyone's like Granny."

In spite of the warning bells clanging in his brain, Dylan grinned right back. "She's not your typical, rocking chair senior citizen?"

"No," Brenna said, laughing.

Dylan felt his gut do a cartwheel and sweat pop out on his upper lip. When Brenna Montgomery let herself, she could be downright devastating. She had the most delightful laugh. And her lips were just meant for kissing.

He frowned. What was wrong with him? She was too unpredictable, too anxious to upset the status quo. She'd not only complained about his uncle Pete's forty year tradition, she'd goaded him into taking her damned class and missing the Tuesday night poker game—a ritual he hadn't missed in the last ten years. Until tonight.

No doubt about it. The lady was trouble. And he'd do well to remember that. He suddenly looked around. The poker game would be breaking up soon. The last thing he needed was for the boys to come out of the back room and start asking why he'd missed the game.

"Is something wrong?" Brenna asked. "All of a sudden you look rather grim."

"Uh…no." Dylan glanced at his watch. "It's getting late. I think we'd better call it a night."

Rising from his chair, he offered his hand. But the moment she placed her hand in his, he knew he'd made a big mistake. Her tender flesh slid along his callused palm like a piece of fine silk, and it took monumental effort on his part not to groan aloud.

He said nothing as he released her hand and followed her out into the night. He couldn't. His mind and body were at war, and it took every bit of his concentration to keep from acting on his first impulse.

Trouble or not, Dylan wanted to take Brenna in his arms and kiss her senseless.

"Where's your car parked?" he asked.

"My grandmother borrowed it for the evening." She glanced at her watch. "But it's probably at home by now." She started down the street. "See you in class next week."

He caught her by the shoulder and turned her to face him. "You walked?"

Nodding, she shrugged out of his grip. "It's not that far."

"It's dark."

"It gets that way at night," she said, dryly. "And that's a problem, because…?"

"It's not safe."

She met his frown with one of her own. "You've just spent the last half hour telling me what a friendly place Tranquillity is. Now you're telling me it's not safe to walk the streets?" She folded her arms and glared up at him. "Make up your mind, Sheriff. What kind of place is this?"

"For the most part, Tranquillity is about as safe as any place can be," he admitted, trying not to stare at the way her full breasts rested on her folded arms. He focused his gaze on the safer area of her forehead. "But once in a while a cowboy from one of the ranches around here gets tanked up and starts to thinking he's Don Juan."

Taking her by the elbow, Dylan hustled her toward his restored '49 Chevy pickup parked across the deserted street. "I've already gotten one complaint from you today. I'd just as soon skip the second."

"No, thanks," she said stubbornly. "I'd rather walk."

He stared down at her. Damn, but she was a feisty

little thing. It was all he could do to keep from kissing her right then and there. Instead, he opened the driver's door, placed his hands at her waist and lifted her into the truck.

She let out an alarmed squeak. "What do you think you're doing?"

"Seeing that you get home safely," he said, climbing in beside her.

"This is totally uncalled for." Glaring at him, she slid over to the passenger side. "I can take care of myself."

"Yeah, sure."

"You can't do this."

"Watch me." He gave her a stern look in an effort to stop any further protest, but she completely ignored it. Blowing out a frustrated breath, he jammed the key into the ignition.

"Are you this controlling with everyone?" she asked.

Dylan tried counting to ten, then twenty. At thirty he gave up. "Lady, you could drive Job over the edge. You complain about an old man's innocent gesture of friendship and then go walking down a dark street at night, inviting all kinds of trouble."

"I do not."

"Yes, you do."

Gunning the engine, he spun gravel and squealed the tires as he steered the truck away from the curb. He cringed as he imagined the chips the rocks had made in the paint job. He and his dad had spent several years restoring the old Chevy, and Jack Chandler was probably looking down from heaven right now, ready to sling a couple of lightning bolts Dylan's way for treating the truck with such irreverence.

He glanced over at the woman beside him. And it was all her fault, too. She was making him crazy and causing him to do things he hadn't done in years. The last time he'd laid rubber had been when he was nineteen and full of more piss and vinegar than good sense.

Fuming, Brenna stared out the passenger window. Dylan was probably right about her walking home alone in the dark, but she'd be darned if she let him know it.

Why did men think they knew what was best for a woman? What made them think that a woman was incapable of making her own decisions?

Tom had always been that way, had always tried to tell her what she should do. And it appeared Dylan Chandler was cut from the same cloth.

When he pulled up in front of her house, she prepared to get out of the truck. "Thank you for the ride. But I have to tell you, your behavior borders on Neanderthal, Sheriff. I—''

"That may be," he interrupted. "But I'm proud to say this caveman can go to bed tonight with a clear conscience." At her raised eyebrow, he had the audacity to grin. "I saw that you got home safe and sound."

"Before you know it, you'll be spouting the code of chivalry, straight from the Round Table," she retorted.

As she reached for the door handle, Dylan caught her wrist and leaned close. "There's nothing wrong with a man protecting a woman from the dangers she's either too naive or too stubborn to recognize for herself.''

''The woman in question might just be a black belt in karate, and able to take care of herself,'' she bluffed, trying to ignore the tingling sensations from his touch, his nearness.

The close confines of the truck cab seemed to grow even smaller and a crazy fluttering started deep in her stomach. His lips were only a few inches from hers. She needed space.

''I appreciate your concern, but—''

''Hush,'' Dylan said, his deep baritone vibrating against her lips a moment before his mouth brushed hers.

At first he teased with featherlight kisses, nibbling, testing her willingness to allow the caress to continue. But when he traced her lips with his tongue, all thought of putting distance between them ceased. Her own tongue automatically darted out to ease the tingling friction of his exploration, but coming into contact with the rough tip of his, the flutters in her stomach went absolutely wild.

At the moment, it didn't seem to matter that she shouldn't be kissing him, tasting him with eager abandon. She was too caught up in the many sensations racing through her to even breathe. When she finally did, the mingled scents of leather, spicy cologne and Dylan caused her nostrils to flare. She didn't think she'd ever smelled anything quite so sensuous, so sexy, so wonderful as the man gathering her to him.

He pulled her unresisting body closer and, trapped between them, her hands clenched his shirt. The firm muscles beneath flexed and bunched at her touch, and his heart pounded against her fingertips. Heat and excitement simultaneously coursed through her when Dylan's tongue penetrated the inner recesses of her mouth. Exploring. Claiming.

Dylan Chandler was the very last man she should be kissing, she thought, her sanity intruding. He was arrogant, controlling and macho from the top of his handsome head, all the way to his big, booted feet. And he was kissing her like she'd never been kissed before.

The intensity of passion might have gotten the better of Dylan, had the steering wheel digging into his ribs not reminded him of where they were. He hadn't necked in the cab of a pickup truck since his senior year in high school. He briefly wished he'd driven the Explorer to town, instead of the truck. It had more room to maneuver. But then, Corny and her hens would have had a field day talking about the sheriff making out in the sheriff's patrol car with the new painting teacher.

Regaining control of his sanity, he leisurely broke the kiss. He'd kissed his share of women, but nothing in his past experience could compare with the wild, untamed feelings he had coursing through him now. He felt like pounding his chest and bench pressing a dump truck.

Hell, he just might have to in order to work off the adrenaline. There were kisses, and then there were *kisses*. And on a scale of one to ten, he'd have to rate this one a fifteen. Maybe even a twenty. Definitely an off-the-scale experience.

His hand shook slightly as he cupped the back of

Brenna's head and gently pressed her cheek to his shoulder. "Wow!"

"That shouldn't have happened," she said breathlessly.

"No, it shouldn't have," he said honestly.

What the hell did he think he was doing? The woman was trouble from the top of her pretty head all the way to her little feet. Hadn't he learned his lesson five years ago?

The best thing he could do would be to see that she got into the house, then get back in his truck and put as many miles between them as the old Chevy would take him.

"I'll walk you to the porch," he said, releasing her.

She reached for the door handle. "It isn't necessary."

But Dylan was out of the cab and around the front of the truck in a flash. When he opened the door and helped her down from the bench seat, he could tell she was going to protest again.

Placing his hand at her back, he ushered her toward the front porch. "My dad made me promise a long time ago that I'd be a gentleman at all times. And that includes walking a lady to the door when I take her home."

"But you were only giving me a ride."

"Doesn't matter," he said stubbornly. "You're a lady. I drove you home. I walk you to the door. It's as simple as that."

When they reached the porch steps, he glanced down at her and felt as if he'd had the wind knocked out of him. This was the way she was meant to look— soft, her hair slightly mussed from having his fingers tangled in the silky strands, a blush of desire coloring her porcelain cheeks.

He had to have lost every ounce of sense he possessed, but he wasn't one bit sorry he was the man to cause that look. His body tightened and he figured it was time to beat a hasty retreat before he did something stupid like kiss her again.

Just as he started to bid her a good evening, the sudden brightness of the porch light made him blink. "What the hell?"

"Brenna? Is that you?"

"You know darned well it is," she muttered, quickly stepping away from him.

An elderly woman around the same age as his uncle Pete, stepped out onto the porch. "Of course I do." The old gal winked at him. "But since it's obvious you aren't going to ask this handsome young man inside, I had to come up with an excuse to meet him."

Removing his hat, Dylan extended his hand. "Dylan Chandler, ma'am. You must be Brenna's grandmother. It's nice to meet you."

"I'm Abigail Montgomery. Won't you come in for a few minutes?" she asked, shaking his hand and treating Brenna to an impish grin.

Brenna gripped the strap on her tote bag so tight she was surprised it didn't snap in two. The smile on her grandmother's face and the delighted twinkle in her eyes promised days of questions, teasing and anything but subtle innuendo.

"Granny, I'm sure Sheriff Chandler has more important matters to attend to." She gave Dylan a pointed look. "Don't you, Sheriff?"

He nodded. "Maybe another time, Mrs. Montgomery."

"I'll hold you to that." Abigail smiled pleasantly. "Maybe Brenna can cook dinner for you some evening."

Brenna couldn't help it. Her mouth dropped open at her grandmother's ridiculous statement.

"Shut your mouth before you catch a bug, kiddo," Abigail advised.

"I'd better say good-night and let you ladies get inside," Dylan said, sounding anxious to make his getaway.

"Thanks again for the ride," Brenna said when her grandmother elbowed her in the ribs.

"No problem," he called, walking out to the truck. "Good night, ladies."

"Night," Abigail said. Once Dylan had started his truck, she steered Brenna through the door. "Let's go inside. You have a lot to tell me. And I'm warning you. This time, I want the straight poop."

"There's nothing to tell," Brenna said, closing the door to secure the lock.

"Oh, yes there is," Abigail shot back. "You told me you didn't like Darren Chancellor."

"Dylan Chandler."

"Whatever," Abigail said, waving her hand. "You told me you had no interest in him."

"I don't."

Abigail snorted. "Yeah, and the Grand Canyon is nothing but a big drainage ditch. Get real."

"Dylan just gave me a ride home." At her grandmother's dubious expression, Brenna added, "He's not my type."

"Sure looked like he is." Abigail laughed delightedly. "It takes some pretty heavy breathing to fog up windows that fast. And I don't blame you one bit. That man's the sexiest stud muffin I've seen come down the pike in a long time."

When her grandmother began humming "Here Comes the Bride," Brenna turned on her heel, walked into her bedroom and slammed the door. She sank down on the side of the bed, rummaged through the drawer of her nightstand and pulled the object of her search from inside. Peeling back the wrapper, she bit into the chocolate bar.

As the rich, smooth taste spread throughout her mouth, she sighed heavily. Life with her grandmother could be trying at best, but now that she'd met Dylan Chandler, it was going to be downright impossible.

Three

———

Dylan rested his chin on his palm and stared off into space. It had been four days since he'd agreed to take Brenna's painting class. Four days since he'd taken her home. And four days that he'd been useless to himself and everyone else.

Oh, he'd gone through the motions of tending to business. But more times than he cared to count, he found himself staring off into space. Like now.

When he'd kissed her, he'd only meant to silence her. But he'd been the one at a loss for words when the kiss ended.

He shook his head as he turned his attention back to the papers on his desk. The last time he'd made the mistake of letting his hormones overrule his good sense he'd come out looking like a complete fool. He had no intention of letting anything like that happen again. And the best way to see that it didn't would be to remove himself from temptation.

Next Tuesday night, instead of going to that damned painting class, he'd be over at Luke's with the rest of the guys doing what they always did— playing poker in the back room.

His decision made, Dylan settled down to the paperwork in front of him. He'd only gotten as far as the middle of the first page when Myron Worthington rushed into his office and plopped his bulk into the chair in front of Dylan's desk.

"We've got big trouble brewin', boy."

"What makes you think that, Myron?" Dylan asked calmly, accustomed to the mayor's excited outbursts.

"Cornelia and them hens of hers are up to somethin'," Myron answered. He fidgeted with his bolo tie every time he talked about his wife, but this time, Dylan thought the man might strangle himself with it.

"You mean the B.S. Club is discussing something more complicated than what refreshments to serve at their next meeting or who they'll get to help them decorate the community room for the Christmas Jamboree?" he asked.

Myron sat forward and nodded vigorously. "This mornin' at breakfast, Cornelia just up and tells me they're gonna redo Main Street in time for the Jamboree, then after that they're gonna do somethin' special for every holiday."

Dylan leaned back, clasped his hands behind his head and propped his boots on the edge of his desk. "Besides holding a weekly meeting, the B.S. Club hasn't done a single thing in the past twenty years besides make cookies and punch for the Christmas Jamboree and decide who they'll coerce into being elves when you play Santa Claus for the kids. What makes you think they'll get anything accomplished in the next month?''

''Because Cornelia told me they already decided to use that artsy-fartsy stuff they're learnin' on Tuesday nights to do it,'' Myron shot back.

Dylan's stomach clenched at the mention of Brenna's painting class. ''Did she tell you what they have planned?''

''No. And that's what's got me worried.'' Myron removed his wide-brimmed Resistol and ran an exasperated hand over his bald head. ''As long as Cornelia's talkin', she ain't doin'. It's when she finally shuts up that you gotta watch out.''

''Did she tell you when they plan to get started?''

Myron shook his head. ''That's where you come in.''

''Me?'' Dylan's boots hit the floor with a thud as he sat up straight. ''What have I got to do with all this?''

''You're takin' that class ain't you?''

''No.''

Myron glared at him. ''Cornelia said you was. She even tried to get me to join in the damned thing.''

Dylan felt heat begin to creep up his neck. ''I was there Tuesday night, but I don't intend to go back.''

''You have to,'' Myron insisted.

The heat spread upward to Dylan's cheeks. ''Why?''

Myron rose from his chair to pace back and forth. ''We have to find out what the B.S. Club's got up their sleeves. And when they plan to get started on it.''

''Just ask your wife,'' Dylan said reasonably.

Myron stopped pacing to peer at him as if he'd sprouted horns and a tail. ''You don't know one damned thing 'bout women, do you, boy?''

Dylan laughed. ''I know enough to get by.''

''I'm not talkin' about snugglin' up to a gal,'' Myron said, exasperated. He tapped his temple with his index finger. ''I'm talkin' about the way they think.''

''How *do* they think, Myron?''

The man splayed his pudgy hands. ''Damned if I know. I've been married to Cornelia for thirty years and I still ain't got her figured out. But I do know when she's got her mind set on somethin', there ain't nothin' or nobody gonna change it. And she's fixed her sights on overhaulin' Main Street.''

''Well, you'll have to get your information some other way,'' Dylan said firmly. ''I don't get along with the teacher.''

''That ought to make it easy then,'' Myron said, looking relieved.

''Forget it, Myron.'' Dylan shook his head. ''I'm not going back to that class.''

Myron gave him a measuring look. ''I don't ever recall havin' to do this, boy. But it looks like there ain't no other way.''

Dylan's stomach twisted into a knot. He knew what the man was driving at. But before he could stop him, Myron announced, ''As the mayor, and your boss, I'm givin' you a direct order to stay in that class and find out what them hens are up to before they make

Tranquillity the laughingstock of the whole damned state.''

Having pronounced sentence, Myron plunked his hat on his shiny, bald pate and walked out of the office with all the authority of a rotund, little monarch.

Dylan propped his elbows on the desk and buried his head in his hands. He didn't like the turn of events one damned bit. The role of spy just wasn't his style. And seeing Brenna every Tuesday night for the next month wasn't going to help him forget that kiss, either.

But orders were orders. He'd always taken pride in his job, and short of resigning as sheriff, Dylan didn't see where he had any other choice.

Brenna took a deep breath, opened the back door and readied herself to face her grandmother once again. Since meeting Dylan four days ago, Abigail had dispensed with any pretense of subtlety and had even gone so far as to try to get Brenna to discuss the number of guests she'd like to invite to the wedding.

"I'm in the living room," Abigail called, when Brenna entered the kitchen. "Come and see who's dropped by for a visit."

Seated beside Abigail on the living room sofa, Pete Winstead treated Brenna to a big grin as he smoothed his mussed hair and replaced his battered cowboy hat. "Nice to see you again, Miss Brenna."

Brenna's eyes widened when her grandmother patted Pete's thigh. "He stopped by to apologize for frightening you the other day,'' Abigail announced. ''Didn't you, Pete?''

''Uh…yeah,'' he agreed. Brenna thought he looked anything but repentant when he added, ''I'm mighty sorry I scared you.''

Abigail rose and walked over to Brenna. ''I can't believe you thought this old goat tried to put the moves on you.'' Eyeing Pete up and down, she looped her arm through Brenna's and gave her a sly grin. ''It's my guess he's too old to have anything but fond memories.''

Brenna's cheeks burned. ''Granny!''

Pete got to his feet, his grin wide. ''Oh, don't you worry nothin' about it, gal.'' He turned his attention to Abigail, took off his hat and pointed to his thick white hair. ''Looks can fool you, sugar. There may be snow on the roof, but there's still one hell of a fire burnin' in the furnace.''

''I wouldn't know about that,'' Abigail shot back. ''I'm not that cold, yet.''

At a loss for words, Brenna looked at her grandmother. Abigail's wrinkled cheeks glowed and her eyes sparkled with mischief. She was having the time of her life.

Pete laughed. ''How 'bout goin' with me to Luke's this evenin', sugar? Some of the men get together on Saturday nights to play their guitars and fiddles. The music ain't too bad and it beats sittin' at home.''

''Doesn't that sound like a hoot?'' Abigail asked Brenna. Turning back to Pete, her voice took on a teasing note. ''We'd love to go. But we're modern women. We'll meet you there.''

Brenna felt like she'd just entered the Twilight

Zone. Not only had Abigail just accepted a date with Pete, she'd included Brenna as part of the package. ''I don't think—''

''Hush, Brenna.'' Abigail hurried Pete toward the door. ''If we don't let this old fossil go, we'll never get ready in time.''

''Old fossil!'' Pete laughed as he stepped out onto the porch. ''I ain't much older than you, sugar. And just wait till tonight. I'll dance your feet plumb off.''

''He'll probably stomp all over them,'' Abigail confided, closing the door. She breezed past Brenna on her way to the bedroom. ''I wonder what the accepted duds are for a place like Kook's?''

''Luke's,'' Brenna corrected. ''The place is called Luke's.''

''Whatever.''

Brenna followed Abigail down the hall. It was just as well her grandmother included her as part of the date. No telling what kind of trouble the geriatric duo would get themselves into.

''Pete thinks he's going to outdance me, but I've got news for the old buzzard. By the time I'm finished with him, his cowboy boots will be smoking.'' Abigail rummaged through her dresser drawers. ''Have you seen my blue scarf?''

''No,'' Brenna said, distracted. She couldn't believe after twenty years of widowhood, Abigail had finally found a man she wanted to see socially.

A sudden thought had her smiling. If her grandmother's mind was on her own love life, she wouldn't have time to concentrate on Brenna's.

As if she could read minds, Abigail stopped searching for the scarf to give Brenna a wicked grin. "Maybe Stud Muffin will be there tonight."

"Give it up, Granny," Brenna said, refusing to believe the sudden flutter in her stomach had anything to do with Abigail's reference to Dylan. "I'm not interested in the man."

Taking a swig of his beer, Dylan listened contentedly to the band play an offbeat version of a George Strait song. Since his talk with the mayor, he'd had time to think, time to put things in perspective about the kiss he'd shared with Brenna. His reaction to her hadn't been all that unusual. It had been a while since he'd enjoyed the warmth of a woman's body, and given the same set of circumstances, a saint would have been tempted.

But the minute he saw Brenna walk through Luke's door, Dylan's mouth went as dry as a desert in a drought. Her pink sweater and designer jeans outlined a body made for sin. The way her hips swayed when she moved made his body tighten and his own jeans feel like they were at least two sizes too small.

Trouble had never looked so good or so tempting. And apparently he wasn't the only man to notice. Several cowboys at the bar nudged each other, their expressions changing from idle curiosity to open appreciation as they watched her cross the room.

Dylan had the inexplicable urge to punch something when one of the men grabbed her by the shoulder. But, bless her heart, Abigail took one look at the guy, whacked him across the knuckles with her handbag, then steered Brenna toward the table Dylan shared with Pete.

"Well, would you look who's here?" Pete declared, a grin spreading across his wrinkled face.

"Brenna, this table only has two chairs. Why don't you and Dillard find yourself one of your own?" Abigail suggested. Her eyes danced merrily as she pointed to the far corner of the room. "That one over in the shadows would give you two the chance to pick up where you left off the other night."

Dylan watched embarrassment stain Brenna's cheeks as several of Luke's patrons turned to openly stare at the old gal's outrageous statement. Something deep inside Dylan's gut twisted and made him want to shelter her from the prying eyes.

"You two kids have fun," Pete said, giving Dylan a meaningful look as he seated Abigail in the chair Dylan had been sitting in.

With the choice taken out of his hands, Dylan touched Brenna's elbow. "It's too noisy to talk here anyway. Let's find a table farther away from the dance floor."

He guided her through the Saturday night crowd and over to an unoccupied table in the corner. Holding the chair for her, he was aware that nearly every eye in the place watched them.

Apparently, the B.S. Club had activated their phone tree after class the other night and spread the word— the sheriff had shown an interest in the new painting teacher. Unfortunately, Abigail had just reinforced the erroneous rumors.

"Need another beer, Dylan?" a young waitress asked as she approached the table.

Dylan smiled at his deputy, Jason's, girlfriend. "I'm fine. Thanks, Susie." Turning his attention to the silent woman beside him, he asked, "Would you like something, Brenna?"

"A diet cola," she murmured quietly.

"Be right back," Susie called over her shoulder as she threaded her way through the tables.

Dylan waited until Brenna's drink arrived before he commented on her somber mood. "You might as well get over it. Your grandmother isn't going to change at this stage of the game."

"You're probably right," Brenna said with a sigh.

Dylan shrugged. "I have the same problem with Uncle Pete. He says what he damned well pleases and to hell with what other people think."

"Granny says it's one of the perks of being older," Brenna agreed. "But I wish she'd use a little more discretion."

He grinned. "I wouldn't count on that happening."

"I suppose you're right," she said, her smile resigned.

After several moments of awkward silence, the band began to play a ballad. Reaching for her hand, Dylan pulled Brenna to her feet. "Let's dance."

He couldn't dance worth a hoot to the faster songs, but he could sway in time to the slower ones. Besides it was better than just staring at each other for the rest of the evening.

But when they reached the dance floor, the crowd swelled and Brenna was pushed against him. Wrapping his arms around her to keep her from falling, Dylan gulped hard. Even though she was quite a bit shorter, she fit him perfectly and his body was already responding in a very X-rated way.

As he held her close, he tried to ignore the feel of

her soft breasts pressed tightly to his chest, the touch of her thighs as they grazed his own. The friction of her lower body rubbing intimately against his caused him to swallow convulsively. Pressed so closely together, there was no way he could hide the fact that he was harder than hell.

Brenna felt the butterflies in her lower abdomen go absolutely wild, and her breath came out in short, little puffs at the feel of Dylan's strong arousal pressed to her lower abdomen. His wide chest blocked out everything around her, and even though they were far from alone, she felt as if they were a million miles from the nearest living soul.

Her arms had automatically encircled his neck when she'd been shoved into him, and she couldn't seem to stop herself from threading her fingers in the thick, ebony hair at his collar. Her eyes drifted shut and she sighed as the soft fabric of Dylan's shirt brushed her cheek. His steely muscles quivered in response to the moist heat of her breath and the movement caused her legs to grow weak.

It would definitely be in her best interest to put some distance between them and seek out a candy machine. Having something chocolate was much safer than wanting to have the sheriff.

His hands caressed the small of her back.

She really should move away.

His lips grazed her temple.

In another moment or two, she'd—

The music stopped suddenly and the room became unnaturally quiet a moment before Pete Winstead's angry voice reverberated across the dance floor. "I said to leave my woman the hell alone, Ira!"

* * *

Dylan's muscles spasmed in protest as he released Brenna and shouldered his way through the crush of people. "What's up, Uncle Pete?" he demanded when he reached the elderly couple.

"This here dog-eared jackass won't leave Abby alone," Pete said, his doubled fist threatening the other man's nose.

"Granny, what's going on?" Brenna asked from behind Dylan.

Abigail's eyes sparkled with excitement. "Isn't this radical?"

"All I wanted was to dance with her," Ira said sullenly, his own fists held in a ready position.

"Then why did you go and call her an old biddy?" Pete asked, his voice accusing.

"I think you both had better settle down," Dylan advised. Mindful of the attention they were drawing from the crowd, he nodded toward the exit. "Let's step outside and see if we can get this straightened out. Ladies?" He held the door as Brenna, Abigail and the two old gentlemen filed past. Once they stood under the neon sign outside Luke's, Dylan turned to Abigail. "What happened, Mrs. Montgomery?"

Abigail pointed to Ira. "This man asked me to dance and I politely refused. When he wouldn't take no for an answer, I told him I preferred a man with a pulse and for him to buzz off. That's when he called me an old biddy."

For having been insulted, Dylan thought Abigail's voice sounded suspiciously pleased. He looked at Ira Jennings and his uncle Pete. Both were seventy and much too old to contemplate a fistfight. Yet here they were, ready to do battle over Abigail. And the old girl was as happy about it as a kid at Christmas.

Dylan's mouth twitched and he struggled to stifle his laughter. Clearing his throat, he tried to sound stern as he stared at the three septuagenarians. ''I should probably run all of you in for disturbing the peace.''

The guilty parties suddenly tried to speak at the same time.

''Now, Dylan, all I wanted was to dance—''

''Whoa, boy! Me and Abby—''

''Pete and I didn't start—''

Dylan placed two fingers to his lips and let loose with a loud, piercing whistle. When the three fell silent, he asked, ''If I let all of you off with a warning, do you think you can go back in there and behave yourselves for the rest of the evening?''

Ira Jennings nodded and beat as hasty a retreat back into the building as his age and arthritis would allow.

Dylan leaned his shoulder against the side of the building and crossed his arms over his chest. ''What about you two?''

Abigail reached for Pete's hand and pulled him along behind her as she headed toward Luke's parking lot. ''We were about to leave anyway.''

''Where are you going?'' Brenna asked.

''Home.'' Abigail continued on to Brenna's car with Pete in tow. Handing him a set of keys, she turned back to wink. ''We're going to make out on the couch.''

''We are?'' Pete asked, his step quickening. Not waiting for an answer, he opened the driver's door and slid inside with a speed that belied his age.

Abigail turned back to Brenna and grinned. ''If there's a handkerchief tied to the front doorknob when you come home, drive around the block a few times.''

''Granny!''

Dylan watched Brenna's cheeks turn a deep shade of rose as she looked around to see if anyone had overheard her grandmother's declaration.

When Pete popped the clutch on the Toyota and spewed gravel as they sped from the parking lot, Dylan pushed away from the building. ''Don't worry. At their age, at least we won't have to worry about a shotgun wedding.''

She stared in the direction the two had disappeared. ''I guess you have a point.''

''Let's go back inside,'' he suggested, holding the door for her.

They hadn't been settled at their table more than ten minutes when Susie tapped him on the shoulder. ''You have a phone call.''

He sighed heavily. The whole evening had been a comedy of errors from the very beginning. ''I suppose Jason told you it was urgent?''

Susie shook her head. ''It isn't Jason.''

''This had better be important,'' Dylan grumbled, making his way to the bar. He covered one ear to block out the rowdy sounds and listened intently. A tight coil of fear twisted his gut a moment before he slammed the receiver back onto its cradle with a succinct curse.

''What is it?'' Brenna asked when he walked back to their table.

"We have to leave." He took her by the elbow and ushered her toward the exit.

"What's wrong?" she asked once they were outside.

The brisk, night air whipped Brenna's hair around her face and she had to trot to keep up with his long strides. He slowed his pace a bit and helped her into the cab when they reached the truck. "You'll see when we get to your place."

Brenna sucked in a sharp breath. "Has something happened to Granny? Or Pete?"

"Yes."

"Which one?"

"Both. They've had a wreck."

"Oh, my God!"

"Pete said they're both all right."

Brenna held on tight as Dylan navigated the deserted streets as if the hounds of hell chased them, and in no time they were slowing down to turn into her drive. When he brought the antique truck to a sliding stop, she gasped at the sight in front of them. One side of the front porch sagged precariously over the crumpled front end of her Toyota.

"Where's Granny and Pete?" she asked, jumping from the cab of Dylan's truck. She reached for her grandmother when the elderly pair stepped from the shadows. "Are you okay?" She looked from Abigail to Pete. "Do either of you need to see a doctor?"

"We're both fine." Abigail hugged Brenna, then pointed to the wreckage. "The car is a little banged up and I think the porch will need a new support post, but it's nothing that can't be fixed."

"How did this happen?" Dylan demanded.

Pete shuffled his feet and stared off into the darkness. "Well...I...that is..."

Abigail winked. "I put my hand on his thigh, and instead of hitting the brake, he floored it. But it doesn't matter now. What's done is done." She looped her arm through Pete's. "We'll go make coffee, while you kids figure out what to do about getting the car off the porch."

"I'm real sorry," Pete said, his blue eyes apologetic.

When the elderly pair walked around to the back of the house, Brenna sighed. "What am I going to do with her? It's like dealing with a teenager."

Staring at the destruction, Dylan shook his head. "It's worse."

Brenna nodded. "I think you're right. It's not like we can ground them or anything."

"I wouldn't want to try." Laughing, he draped a companionable arm across her shoulders. "Let's see what kind of damage the two delinquents have left in their wake and what we'll have to do in order to fix it."

Four

Brenna had just put the finishing touches to the black Geisha girl wig when Abigail tapped lightly on the bedroom door. "Studly's here."

"Who?"

Abigail grinned. "Dylan."

"Why?"

Her grandmother walked over and plopped down on the edge of the bed. "It's my guess he has the hots for you."

"Please tell me you didn't ask him to give me a ride to the school," Brenna pleaded.

"Nope." Abigail smiled beatifically. "Bright boy, that Dylan Chandler. It was all his idea. He said since Pete wrecked your car it was only right that he drive you to work until it's repaired."

The thought of seeing Dylan again made Brenna's pulse quicken. And that wasn't good. Not good at all.

Since her ill-fated relationship with Tom ended almost a year ago, she'd been very careful to avoid becoming involved with another man. And especially one like Dylan Chandler.

His take-charge personality made her nervous and reminded her of why she'd moved to Texas in the first place. She was making a fresh start, becoming a new, self-assured woman who controlled her own life and made her own choices. Never again would she allow a man to manipulate her into doing what he wanted or what he thought was best for her.

Dylan's decision to drive her to the grade school for story hour might be a minor point, but it was an important one. Instead of asking her if she wanted him to give her a ride, he'd just assumed that she would go along with his plan.

"Tell him thanks, but I prefer to walk. I need the exercise."

"Oh, cellulite be damned." Abigail jerked her thumb at the window. "There's a good-looking man out there who obviously wants to be with you, and if you don't get the lead out, you're going to be late anyway."

Brenna glanced at her watch and cursed herself for hitting the snooze button on her alarm one too many times. If she didn't hurry, the Story Lady would be the second graders least favorite person in about ten minutes.

"Tell Dylan I'll be right out," she said, deciding that whether she liked it or not, accepting a ride to the school was the only way she'd arrive on time.

"Outstanding decision." Abigail smiled triumphantly as she headed for the door. "It's a relief to know I didn't raise a total ditz."

Brenna ignored her grandmother's comment and hurriedly gathered her bag of craft supplies and the book she'd chosen to read to the children. Glancing at herself in the mirror on the back of her closet door to make sure her kimono was straight, she shook her head. "It's no big deal. You're not interested in him. He's just giving you a ride to the school. Nothing more."

But when she stepped outside and spied Dylan leaning against the fender of a black-and-white SUV with Sheriff's Patrol painted on the sides, her pulse fluttered and she had an almost uncontrollable urge to dig through her handbag for a chocolate bar.

He was wearing aviator sunglasses and a black leather bomber jacket. Combined with his black cowboy hat and snug jeans, he looked better than any man had the right to look. And especially at eight in the morning.

As Brenna approached, Dylan unfolded his arms to point to her costume. "Why do you wear those get-ups?"

"The children enjoy seeing costumes that go along with the stories I read and the crafts we make afterward." Her eyes narrowed. "You have a problem with that…Sheriff?"

"None at all," Dylan lied, opening the passenger door. He couldn't tell her that whether she represented a truckload of trouble or not, he hated seeing her luscious curves covered up with the outlandish garbs. She wouldn't appreciate it one bit. Hell, he wasn't even comfortable with the way he felt about it himself. "What time do you close your shop this afternoon?"

"Five." She hitched her kimono up to her knees and climbed into the Explorer. "Why?"

When he caught sight of her shapely legs, he had to swallow several times before he finally managed, "I'll be by to give you a ride home." Walking around the front of the vehicle, he slid behind the wheel, then radioing his deputy that he would return to the office in a few minutes, signed off.

"Thank you for the offer. I really appreciate it. But I prefer to walk," she said, sounding quite firm about the matter. "I'm getting soft in my old age and I need the exercise."

"You're not old." He backed the SUV out onto the street, then let his gaze travel from her pretty face to her little feet. Before he could stop himself, he added, "And soft is nice. Real nice."

Her cheeks colored a pretty pink. "Dylan—"

The sudden crackle of the police radio, followed by his deputy's excited voice, intruded. "Dylan, Mayor Worthington is here to see you and he's as mad as an old wet hen."

Dylan cursed and reached for the radio's microphone. "Calm down, Jason. Get Myron a cup of coffee and tell him to relax. I'll be there in five minutes."

He replaced the handheld mike and drove the distance to the grade school in silence. What the hell had he been thinking when he told her he liked her softness? If Jason hadn't interrupted him, there was no telling what he would have ended up saying.

And why was he insisting on taking her home this

afternoon? Why did it bother him that she preferred to walk, rather than accept a ride with him?

He should be down on his hands and knees thanking the good Lord above that she had the good sense to turn him down. But the memory of how she'd felt in his arms when they'd danced at Luke's the other night, the taste of her sweet lips beneath his when he'd brought her home from painting class, had haunted him for the better part of a week. And whether it was smart or not, Dylan wanted to feel her soft curves against his body once again, wanted to kiss her until they both required oxygen.

"I'll see you at five," he said, pulling to a stop in front of the school.

"I'd rather—"

"This isn't negotiable. I'll take you home," he said. Unable to stop himself, he reached out to gently run the back of his hand along the side of her soft cheek. "Do you need a ride from the school to your shop after story hour?"

"No, it's only a couple of blocks," she said, sounding breathless.

Satisfied that she wasn't going to protest further, he smiled as she got out of the truck. "I'll see you this afternoon, Brenna."

Dylan watched Myron bluster and sputter about the Beautification Society's latest scheme to improve the town, and he had to admit the excitable little man had a valid point. "Myron, I agree with you one hundred percent. But I don't think you have anything to worry about."

Myron stopped his pacing to peer at Dylan as if

he'd sprouted another head. "Boy, ain't you heard a word I've said? Cornelia and them hens of hers are fixin' to turn this town into a laughingstock. Hell. We'll probably be the biggest joke in Texas."

Dylan calmly left his chair to pour himself and Myron another cup of coffee. "The only way it can happen is if they get the store owners to go along with the idea. And what chance do you think they'll have with Luke Washburn or Ed Taylor? Can you honestly say you think they'll replace their neon signs with painted, wooden ones?"

The rotund little mayor sat down heavily in the chair across from Dylan's desk. "I guess you're right. It's just that I know Cornelia. Once she sets her mind to something, ain't nothin' or nobody gonna change it."

"In this case, she'll have to." Dylan returned to his chair. Leaning back, he propped his boots on the edge of the desk. "If the store owners don't want to change their signs, there's no way the B.S. Club can force the issue."

"I sure as hell hope not." Myron thoughtfully sipped his coffee. "I noticed you and that little Montgomery gal were at Luke's Saturday night. Did you find out anything?"

Dylan shook his head warily as he watched the mayor take another sip. Myron's beady little eyes peering at him over the edge of the coffee mug made the hair on the back of Dylan's neck crawl and reminded him of the way a rattlesnake looked just before it strikes.

"You two seem to be mighty friendly," Myron said, giving him a smile that caused Dylan to grind his back teeth. "That might be a good way to find out what we need to know."

"You can forget that angle, Myron." Dylan narrowed his eyes to let the man know he meant business. "We both happened to be at Luke's and shared a dance. Nothing more. Besides, Brenna has nothing to do with the B.S. Club or any of their hare-brained schemes."

Long after the mayor left his office, Dylan stared off into space. He didn't like that Myron or anyone else would even suggest that he see Brenna in order to gain information about the B.S. Club. Dylan had something similar happen to him a few years back and he knew exactly how it felt to be used to further someone's cause.

Thinking back on that time, he still couldn't believe what a fool he'd been. He'd fallen hook, line and sinker for the beautiful young woman who had breezed into Tranquillity on the pretense of buying property to open a bed-and-breakfast. But he'd found out the hard way she was only using his attraction to her in order to gain information she needed about the town for a much bigger venture.

He'd quickly learned how much he meant to her when she showed up at a town council meeting and revealed that she'd been collecting facts and figures for a development deal that would have turned Tranquillity into a resort for the rich to "get back to nature." She'd thrown out statistics and talked about how the town should capitalize on its location at the base of the Davis Mountains. She'd pressed the councilmen to pass zoning laws requiring the shop owners along Main Street to upgrade their businesses or close their doors. And had she been successful, the cost of living in Tranquillity would have skyrocketed, making it impossible for the longtime residents to afford to stay there.

But the worst of it had been when she indicated that Dylan supported the changes and the new resort her development firm intended to build at the edge of town. She'd even gone so far as to pull out a nice, fat check for his part in the research and feasibility study, and tried to give it to him in front of Myron and the rest of the council. That's when all hell broke loose.

The council rejected her proposal outright and she'd left town without a backward glance. But the damage had been done. Dylan's reputation with the people of Tranquillity, not to mention his ego, had taken a hell of a beating that night. And for the first time in his life, his integrity had been thrown into question.

It had taken him months to regain the town's trust and respect, and there wasn't a snowball's chance in hell that he'd ever treat anyone to that brand of humiliation or betray their trust in such a callous manner. And especially not Brenna.

Dylan shook his head. It was a moot point anyway. She wasn't a member of the B.S. Club and had no knowledge of what the old hens were up to.

He reached inside his desk drawer to pull out the list of supplies for Brenna's class. He'd follow orders and go through the motions of learning to paint. If he overheard the women talking about the project, he'd tell Myron. And if he didn't, the mayor would just have to gain the information he wanted elsewhere.

But either way, Dylan had every intention of distancing himself from the whole situation as soon as possible.

Dylan entered Brenna's craft store about fifteen minutes before closing and stopped dead in his tracks. Several things about her seemed to register with him all at once. She'd changed from the Oriental costume she'd worn that morning into a pair of jeans and a long-sleeved, forest-green T-shirt. She'd taken off the Japanese-styled, black wig and her long copper hair hung in a single braid down the middle of her back. But most of all, he noticed how her little rump looked when she bent over to help old Mrs. Pennington with something on the bottom shelf of a wall filled with skeins of yarn. Damn, but Brenna had a fine-looking rear end.

The bell over the door had alerted her of his arrival, and looking over her shoulder, she smiled. "Is it five already?"

He shrugged as he tried to get his vocal cords to work. "Close enough," he finally managed. "Where would I find the supplies for the painting class?"

She pointed to a shelf filled with paints, brushes and wood cut into all kinds of shapes. "Everything you'll need is grouped together by project. If you need help, just let me know."

Dylan nodded, then forced his feet to move in the direction she'd indicated. He needed help all right, but not the kind she was talking about. The sight of her delightful bottom had his heart pounding against his rib cage like a jungle drum and had brought him to full arousal so fast he felt light-headed.

Picking up a basket, he held it in front of him and tried to will himself to calm down as he filled it with little plastic bottles of acrylic paint. If he didn't get hold of himself, and damned quick, he'd be a raving lunatic in short order.

"Are you finding everything you need?" she asked from beside him.

He looked around. Mrs. Pennington was gone and they were alone. Why hadn't he heard the bell over the door when the elderly woman left, or the sound of Brenna's approach?

"I'm pretty sure I have everything on the list," he said, holding out the basket for her inspection.

She gazed at the items, then smiled. "Looks like you're right."

When she reached out to take hold of the handle her hand brushed his and Dylan felt a streak of electricity run up his arm, then down through his chest and straight to his groin. It took every ounce of willpower he possessed to keep from dropping the basket, pulling her into his arms and kissing her as senseless as he felt.

They stared at each other for several long seconds before she took the basket from him. "I'll start totaling these so we can get out of here." She walked behind the counter to remove the supplies from the basket. "How was your day?"

Thinking of his meeting with Myron helped Dylan get his mind off the gentle sway of her hips and back to the reason he was buying painting supplies in the first place. "I've had better."

"I'm sure it couldn't have been all that bad," she

said, smiling up at him. "Things will probably look a lot different tomorrow."

That all depends on who's doing the looking.

"Maybe," he said, trying not to think about how pretty she was, or how soft and sweet her voice sounded. He reached into his hip pocket for his wallet, removed a couple of bills and handed them to her. "We've talked about my day. How was yours?"

"Pretty fantastic," she said, pressing the buttons to total out the cash register. "Mrs. Worthington came by this afternoon with the most marvelous idea. She and the ladies of the Beautification Society have asked me to join the organization and head the project to decorate Main Street for the holidays. Isn't that wonderful?"

Dylan felt like his heart landed on top of his boots. "Sure." It's just downright peachy, he thought sourly.

"You look awfully grim. Is something wrong?"

"No." He hadn't intended for the word to come out quite so quickly or with such force. But why did she have to go and join old Corny and her hens, and in the process, complicate his life that much more?

"I'm a good listener. Would you like to talk about what's bothering you?" she asked as she placed his painting supplies into a sack. "Sometimes it helps to get it out, put it behind you and move on."

"Not really."

If he told her about the mayor ordering him to remain in her class, in order to find out what the B.S. Club had up their sleeves, it would get things out and put something *behind* him all right—her foot behind him as she kicked his sorry butt *out* the door.

"If you change your mind, the offer stands," she said, with a shrug. She walked around the room, turning off lights over display cases. "Oh, by the way, Granny called this afternoon. She wanted me to tell you that she and Pete took your truck and drove down to Alpine for dinner and a movie."

"That's just great," Dylan said sarcastically. "It was Pete's turn to cook."

"I guess I could fix something for both of us," Brenna said, looking uncertain.

His mood lightened considerably and he smiled for the first time since entering her shop. "That would be nice."

He had no intention of questioning her. But if she volunteered information about the B.S. Club's plans, he could tell Myron, then drop out of her class with a clear conscience.

But watching Brenna gather her purse and tote bag, he felt as if a weight settled over his shoulders. Why did the idea of not seeing her every Tuesday night bother him?

"Do you need help?" Dylan asked when they entered the house Brenna shared with her grandmother.

She shook her head as she turned on the television. "Why don't you relax and watch the news while I get things started?"

When she left him alone, Dylan took off his hat and looked around the small, comfortably furnished room. From the ruffled curtains at the windows, to the lace doilies on the fragile-looking end tables, everything looked so feminine, he felt like a bull in a china shop.

Amused, he shook his head. Brenna's house was nothing like the rustic cabin he shared with Pete—a place where a man wasn't afraid to sit down.

A delicate, antique curio cabinet with a collection of porcelain cherubs, some of which looked quite old, drew Dylan's attention and he walked over to take a look. Nestled among the figurines a brass frame displayed the photograph of a man and woman, their arms around each other.

"My mother and father," Brenna said quietly, walking up to stand beside him. "That picture was taken shortly before their deaths."

"What happened?"

"They were killed in a car accident almost ten years ago. When I was fifteen," she said quietly.

His gut twisted into a tight knot at the haunted shadows clouding her wide blue eyes and the sadness in her soft voice. Without a second thought, he turned and took her into his arms.

He told himself he was only lending her comfort. But to be perfectly honest, he'd wanted to hold her body to his, to feel her breasts pressed to his chest since they'd danced together the other night at Luke's.

When she wrapped her arms around his waist, he rested his cheek against the top of her head and they stood silently for several moments.

"What about your folks, Dylan?" she finally asked.

The sound of his name on her velvet voice did strange things to his insides. "Mom died when I was in college and Dad passed away about five years ago."

"You're an only child, too?"

He nodded. "My mother found out she was pregnant with me on her fortieth birthday, right after they'd given up any hope of ever having kids."

Brenna pulled back to smile at him. "And look what they wound up with."

He understood her need to lighten the mood. "What they wound up with is getting hungry, lady," he said, laughing. He turned her loose, then stepped back. "When do we eat?"

Brenna took a deep breath. The moment of truth had arrived. She was going to have to go into the kitchen and give it her best shot. Or tell Dylan the truth and call for a pizza.

"I guess I'd better get started on dinner before you waste away to nothing."

"I'll help," he offered, following her.

Walking to the refrigerator, she opened the door and stared inside as if the answer to her dilemma would somehow magically be revealed. Nothing materialized. Spying a carton of eggs, she hesitated. Her grandmother had always said anyone could make an omelette. She sure hoped Abigail was right.

"How does an omelette sound?" Brenna asked, hopefully.

"Great." He rubbed his hands together. "Give me a knife and I'll dice up whatever you have for the filling."

"Filling?"

"Yeah, the stuff that goes inside, like ham, cheese, peppers…." He frowned. "You have made omelettes before, haven't you?"

"Uh…sure," Brenna lied. "Why don't you relax

and watch television, or read the newspaper while I whip these up?''

''Are you sure?''

''Of course.'' She had to get him out of the kitchen so she could search for her grandmother's cookbook. ''You've had a hard day and it won't take long for me to get these baked.''

He frowned. ''Baked?''

''Cooked,'' she said quickly. ''I meant cooked.''

A sudden wave of panic swept through her as she watched him shrug and walk back into the living room. Her culinary skills barely included boiling water to make a cup of tea. What on earth had she been thinking when she'd offered to cook for them?

She stood motionless for a moment as she stared at the cabinets. Then spinning into action, she searched first one cabinet, then another for Abigail's cookbook. Where had her grandmother put the darned thing?

When Brenna finally found the tattered book, she breathed a sigh of relief. ''Omelettes,'' she muttered, running her finger down the index. ''Where are the recipes for omelettes?''

Dylan listened to the sounds coming from the kitchen over the low volume of the television. It sounded like a small war had broken out. Pans clattered and cabinet doors banged as Brenna moved around the compact kitchen. A loud splat followed by a heartfelt *damn* had him rising halfway out of the chair.

''Are you sure you don't need help?'' he called.

''Everything's under control.''

Uneasy about the strange sounds coming from the kitchen, he settled back into the chair. If things were fine, why did she sound so flustered? And why was she making all that noise?

A panicked shriek, followed closely by the screech of a smoke detector, suddenly caused the hair on the back of his neck to stand straight up, and a chill to race the length of his spine. Bolting from the chair, he collided with Brenna as she ran from the kitchen.

"What the hell's going on?" he demanded.

"The kitchen is on fire!"

He pushed past her and into the dense smoke that was rapidly filling the room. Flames licked at the bottom of a small skillet and a dark cloud of smoke billowed from the top of the electric range.

"Do you have a fire extinguisher?"

She coughed and pointed to the cabinet under the sink. "In there."

Dylan quickly located the red cylinder strapped to the inside of the cabinet, jerked it loose, took aim and squeezed the handle. A cloud of white vapor instantly and efficiently put out the flame.

"Are you all right?" he asked when he turned to face her. His voice sounded more harsh than he'd intended, but the woman had scared him out of a good ten years of life.

His concern increased when Brenna stood silently in the doorway, tears streaming down her red face. Had she suffered a burn?

He walked over to her and searched for any signs that she'd been injured. When he found none, he took her into his arms. "How in the hell did you manage to set an electric stove on fire?"

"I have no idea." Obviously embarrassed to tears, she buried her face against his chest and wailed, "I don't know the first thing about cooking."

An empty pizza box between them, Dylan and Brenna sat cross-legged on the living room floor. They'd scrubbed down the range top and washed the skillet, but an acrid scorched scent still lingered throughout the house.

"I wish we could get the smell out of here," she said, wrinkling her nose.

She watched him move the box to the side, stretch his legs out in front of him, then lean back on one elbow. "That's going to take some time. You really had the smoke rolling in there, darlin'."

When she noticed his inquisitive look, she sighed. "I suppose you want to know why I didn't tell you I'm one of the cooking impaired."

He nodded and the corner of his mouth twitched suspiciously, as if he were trying to keep from grinning.

"I didn't think cooking an omelette would be *that* hard," she said defensively.

"It's not."

"And I suppose you know how to cook?"

"Sure do," he said, his grin breaking through.

"I might have known." She frowned. "And you're probably good at it, too."

"As a matter of fact, I am," he said, chuckling. He reached out and took her hand, then pulled her down onto the thick carpet beside him. "But I'm much better at other things," he said, his drawl so warm and sexy that a shiver slid down her spine.

Her breath caught at the smoldering look in his eyes. He was going to kiss her again, and the thought both thrilled her and scared her to death at the same time.

"Dylan, I don't think—"

He placed his index finger to her lips. "I'm not thinking right now either," he said, lowering his head.

She tried to remind herself he was all wrong for her, that he was too macho, too controlling. But the moment his firm lips settled over hers, none of that seemed to matter.

Caught up in the maelstrom of sensation, she decided that whether it was wise or not, she wanted his kiss. She wanted him to once again make her aware of the differences between them, the complementing contrast of man to woman.

She reveled in his strength, the feel of his strong arms cradling her to him, his muscular legs tangled with hers. As his lips leisurely caressed hers that fluttery feeling in the pit of her stomach took off at a gallop. But when Dylan parted her lips to deepen the kiss, the fluttering intensified, tightened and transformed into the sweet ache of pure desire.

Tiny jolts of electric current skipped along Brenna's nerve endings as Dylan's hands tangled in her hair. He pressed his hard length to her and the groan of pleasure rumbling up from deep in his chest, sent an answering need spreading throughout her body.

"Well now. This explains why the house smells like smoke, Abby," Brenna heard Pete say. "Looks like the kids are playin' with fire."

"Or Brenna's been trying to cook again," her grandmother said.

The sensual fog around Brenna disappeared in an instant.

"To tell you the truth, it's a combination of both," Dylan said, raising his head to look up at them.

Brenna pushed against Dylan's wide chest. Thank goodness, her grandmother and Pete had shown up before she did something stupid.

But the sight of the elderly couple's *we-know-what-you've-been-doing* smiles had her immediately trying to bury her face in Dylan's wide chest, and wishing with all her heart that she could get her hands on a Hershey bar.

Five

His mind occupied with the gentle sway of Brenna's hips as she moved from table to table around the community room, Dylan failed to catch what the woman next to him had said. "What's that, Mildred?"

She pointed to the streak of paint that looked like a big, fat comma on the wooden plaque he was painting. "I said, you do the brush strokes so well that you should think about helping the Beautification Society with our Main Street Project."

His left eyebrow twitched at the mention of the B.S. Club's project. "I don't think that would be a good idea, Mildred," he said, careful to keep his voice low. "The guys over at Luke's—"

"Oh, how silly of me," Mildred interrupted with a laugh. She placed her wrinkled hand on his arm, her expression sympathetic. "Of course, you wouldn't be able to help. The Beautification Society is a women's organization. I forgot about you being a man.''

Nodding, Dylan managed a smile that probably looked more like a grimace before turning his attention back to his painting. How much more was his ego supposed to endure for the sake of the town anyway? Not only had the guys over at Luke's given him a hard time about taking a damned painting class with old Corny and her hens, he'd just been neutered by a sweet little sixty-year-old lady he'd known all of his life.

''You're doing a wonderful job, Dylan. I'm very impressed with your progress.''

At the sound of Brenna's soft voice, he raised his head and anything he might have said about not giving a damn whether he was good at the technique or not, lodged in his throat. The smile she gave him was so encouraging, he forgot all about the guys over at Luke's or that he'd just been stripped of his gender by Mildred. All he could think of was how soft Brenna's lips looked and how he'd like nothing more than to taste them again, to feel them beneath his as he kissed her.

''Would you like to go over to Luke's for a cup of coffee after class?'' he blurted out without thinking of where he was, or that he had an audience.

The background buzz of female voices suddenly stopped as if they awaited Brenna's answer, and when he glanced around the room, Dylan barely controlled the urge to squirm. The knowing smiles on the women's faces sent heat creeping up his neck to spread across his cheeks. He'd just the same as announced an interest in Brenna to an entire roomful of world-class gossips.

But as the women continued to grin at him, he decided there was no sense denying it any longer—not to himself or anyone else. He *was* interested in Brenna and not because he'd been ordered to take her class, or for the information she might pass on about the B.S. Club project.

Whether he liked it or not, the more he was around Brenna, the more he wanted to know about her, and the more he wanted to explore the attraction that seemed to draw them together like a magnet. He'd just have to make sure he kept it casual. That shouldn't be difficult, he decided.

Coming to terms with the realization, and his decision, he grinned back at the roomful of women, not giving a damn what they thought. "So what do you say?" he asked, turning his attention back to Brenna. "Want to go for coffee after class?"

Her cheeks colored a pretty pink as she glared at him. "I don't think—"

Before Brenna could finish turning him down, old Corny came to his rescue by jumping to her feet and announcing, "Girls, it's time to quit for the evening."

He watched Brenna look helplessly around the room at the women gathering their painting supplies. "But class isn't over. We still have another fifteen minutes, ladies."

"Brenna, dear, will you be available tomorrow evening for a meeting of the Beautification Society's planning committee?" Cornelia asked as she hurriedly stuffed bottles of acrylic paint into a small box.

As Brenna's disapproving expression turned to anticipation, a tight knot formed in the pit of Dylan's belly and his eyebrow twitched. He could tell she not only looked forward to being part of the Main Street Project, she was eager to get started.

"What time should I be here, Mrs. Worthington?" she asked.

"Seven is our usual meeting time," Corny said, picking up the basket of painting supplies and heading for the door. The old gal stopped to send a wink his way. "The meeting will be over around eight-thirty, in case someone wants to give her a ride home, Dylan."

"I'll remember that," he said, grinning back at the older woman.

The women cleared the room in record time, and when the last one closed the door behind her, Brenna turned to glare at Dylan. "I hope you're happy, Sheriff. You've single-handedly destroyed my first Folk Art class."

"Nope." His unrepentant grin took her by surprise. "As far as I could tell, it was a huge success."

"How can you say that?" she asked incredulously. "Everyone left before they'd completed the project."

He stood, then rounding the table, stopped in front of her. "Anything that can keep Cornelia Worthington as quiet as she was this evening when she practiced the painting techniques you taught, is nothing short of miraculous."

His sexy smile and the rhythm of his deep voice made Brenna's heart skip a beat. But when he reached out to draw her into his arms, she shook her head to clear it. "Dylan, this isn't a good idea."

"What?" he asked, pulling her close.

"You. Me." His lips brushed hers, sending a wave of shivers coursing through her. "I don't think it's…wise."

"Darlin', whether it's wise or not, it's not going to go away."

He nibbled kisses along her jawline to the hollow of her ear, and instead of pushing him away, she wrapped her arms around his waist. "It might."

His deep chuckle caused her pulse to race. "I don't think so, Brenna. I've tried ignoring it for the past week and it's just gotten stronger."

"Try harder," she said, wondering if the community center had candy machines with a good selection of chocolate bars.

"Do you really want me to do that, darlin'?" he asked, nuzzling the sensitive skin along the side of her neck.

"Yes." Even she could detect the lack of conviction in her tone.

"Liar." He leaned back to look down at her and the heat in his gaze took her breath. "I'm going to kiss you, Brenna. And afterward, I want you to look me in the eyes and tell me you don't feel something drawing us together."

Before she could protest, he lowered his mouth to hers and she felt every ounce of her resistance drain away. Even the intense desire for something chocolate to sooth her jangled nerves faded to nothingness as she melted against him.

He caught her to his wide chest, then ran his hands from her back down to cup her bottom in his large hands. Lifting her to him, he let her feel his strong arousal at the same time he parted her lips with a thrust of his tongue. It felt as if a herd of butterflies were suddenly set free inside her lower stomach. As he stroked, tasted and explored her with a mastery that made her lightheaded, the fluttering tightened into a coil of deep need and Brenna had to cling to his strong biceps for support.

Dylan eased the kiss in slow degrees and by the time he lifted his mouth from hers, she felt as if her world had changed and nothing would ever be the same again. Whether she liked it or not, there was no denying the truth any longer. Maybe it was chemistry. Maybe it was magnetism. She wasn't sure. But whatever it was called, there was something between her and Dylan that was far more explosive than anything she'd ever shared with Tom. And it scared the daylights out of her.

"Now, tell me you didn't feel that, too," Dylan said, resting his forehead against hers.

"I…I'd be lying if I told you I didn't feel anything," she said shakily. "But I won't give up my independence or my identity for the opportunity to find out what it is. I won't give another man that kind of power over me ever again."

Brenna suddenly clamped her lips together and when she looked up at him, the shadows in her expressive blue eyes caused a knot to form in Dylan's gut. "Who did this to you, darlin'?"

Her gaze skittered away. "Did what?"

"Who gave you the idea that men want to control women, want them to be dependent?" he demanded. If he could get his hands on the man who gave her that impression, Dylan would cheerfully throttle the stupid jerk.

"It's…not important," she said, pulling herself from his arms. "Just suffice it to say, I learned my lesson well."

"Dammit, Brenna, it is important," Dylan said, reaching out to place his hands on her shoulders. "If I'm being compared to another man, I'd like to know why."

Just when he thought she was going to ignore his request, she took a deep breath. "I met Tom in my senior year in college. He was a struggling law student and I was well on my way to a degree in business administration. To make a long story short, we started seeing each other and fell in love." She shook her head. "That's not right. I thought I was in love and he thought that gave him the right to manipulate and control me."

"What do you mean?"

She sighed heavily. "Over time, he convinced me to dress a certain way, told me how I should wear my hair and when I should go on a diet." When she laughed, the self-deprecating sound caused Dylan to wince. "I was naive and wanted to please the man I loved, so I went along with the changes. Then after I graduated, he even talked me into helping him financially with his last year of law school."

Dylan felt his chest tighten. He had a good idea what was coming next and he didn't like it one damned bit. "How long before—"

"Before he dumped me?"

"I wasn't going to put it that way," Dylan said gently. She looked so vulnerable, he pulled her back into his arms.

"You might as well put it that way," she said,

shrugging. "Because that's exactly what happened—right after he passed the bar." She pulled back to look up at him. "I trusted Tom when he said the money I gave him for his schooling was an investment in our future."

Dylan's gut twisted into a tight knot at the pain and humiliation the conniving jerk had caused Brenna. If he could have gotten his hands on this Tom character at that very moment, Dylan would have made the bum sorry he'd ever been born.

Cupping her face with his hands, Dylan gazed into her pretty blue eyes. "Darlin', I promise you that's one thing you'll never have to worry about with me. I'm not a control freak. I like you just the way you are. And I don't want anything more from you than the pleasure of your company."

She stared up at him for several long seconds before she stepped back, then walked to the front of the room to pack her tote bag. They had more in common than he would have thought. Apparently he wasn't the only one with a past he'd rather not repeat.

Walking up behind her, Dylan wrapped his arms around her midriff, then leaned down to whisper in her ear. "Let's just take this one step at a time and see what happens."

"But—"

"One step at a time, darlin'." He turned her to face him. "But I think I'd better warn you. I have every intention of asking you to go with me to Luke's Saturday night." Smiling, he took a step back to keep her from feeling crowded. "You know, I think I'm going to live dangerously tonight and have a piece of apple pie with my coffee. How about you?"

She looked thoughtful for a moment before she finally asked, "Do you think Luke would happen to have a slice of chocolate pie in that pie case?"

The first Saturday in December, Brenna waited for the members of the Beautification Society to gather around her on the sidewalk in front of her craft store. Fortunately, winters in southwest Texas were very mild and today was testament to how beautiful the weather could be. The sun was shining brightly, the temperature was in the upper sixties and humidity was almost nonexistent—ideal weather for paint to dry.

"Okay, ladies, I think it would be best to work in pairs," she said, checking her list. She glanced up to count the number of women who had shown up for the first phase of the Main Street Project. "Mildred, you have a notation here that one side of Main Street has an extra hydrant."

Mildred Bruner stepped forward as she hitched up her patched blue jeans. "That's right. There's one on the west side that's stuck in the middle of the block." Her cackling laughter broke the early morning silence as she pointed down the street. "Right in front of the Fire Department and Sheriff's office."

Brenna laughed. "I don't guess it would do for the Fire Department to catch fire." She glanced at her clipboard again. "We have enough teams to do all of them, except for that one. I suppose I could paint it after I get everyone else started."

"Oh, that's a marvelous idea, since you and Dylan are courting," Mrs. Worthington said excitedly. "Don't you think it would be appropriate to put a star on that one's chest and make it look like Dylan in a Santa suit?''

"I think that's a great idea," one of the women said, causing the entire group to nod their heads in eager agreement.

Brenna smiled wanly. If her grandmother's comments about her seeing Dylan weren't enough, now the women of Tranquillity were jumping on the bandwagon. But she was reasonably sure they wouldn't be taking it to the extreme her grandmother had. Just that morning, before Brenna left to start the first phase of the Main Street Project, Abigail had gone so far as to ask what flavor of punch Brenna preferred for the wedding reception.

"I think painting the fire hydrants like our men in Santa suits is a fantastic idea," Emily Taylor said. She gave Brenna a sly grin, then pointed down the block. "I intend to make the one in front of our hardware store look just like my Ed."

Helen Washburn nodded vigorously. "And I'll paint the one in front of our place to look like Luke." She glanced at her watch. "Brenna, do you really think we can get all these done today?"

"That's the plan," Brenna said, smiling.

"Oh, good," Helen said, clearly excited. "It being Saturday and all, everyone will be coming to the dance at our place tonight. It's going to be the perfect opportunity to show off the first phase of our Christmas project."

"Then let's begin," Cornelia said, grabbing a box filled with jars of paint and brushes. "Brenna, dear, how should we go about this?"

"Everyone choose a painting partner," Brenna instructed the eager women. "While one of you works on the front of the hydrant, the other should work on the back."

Brenna watched the ladies of the Tranquillity Beautification Society set to work with more enthusiasm than expertise, turning ordinary fire hydrants into works of Christmas art. After making sure everything was going smoothly, she picked up her own paint kit and headed for the hydrant in front of Dylan's office.

She worked quickly and, in no time, had the details roughed in. Her eyes held an impish gleam as she used the liner brush to add the finishing touches. It was an absolute shame she couldn't put a red fur Santa's hat on the little guy, instead of having to paint one on.

"Dear, you've done an excellent job of capturing Dylan's likeness." Cornelia pushed a strand of blue-gray hair from her eyes as she peered at Brenna's work, then glanced at the door of the Sheriff's office. "By the way, where is Dylan? Shouldn't he be on duty?"

"He's gone up into the mountains to help search for a couple of lost hikers," Brenna answered. She finished painting a silver star on the chest of the Santa Claus hydrant. "He probably won't be back until late this afternoon or evening. But Jason is in charge if you need something."

"No." Lowering her voice for privacy, Cornelia asked, "Has Dylan mentioned what he thinks of the Beautification Society's plans to decorate Main Street for the Jamboree?"

The tone in the older woman's voice caused Brenna

to glance up from her work. Seeing the woman's grave expression, Brenna rose to face her.

"He knows the Society have some improvements planned, but I haven't shared any of the details. Why?"

"I just wondered." Cornelia heaved a sigh. "Last night, Myron almost suffered apoplexy when I told him that the first phase would begin today."

Brenna smiled as she gazed down at the hydrant she'd just finished painting. "I'm sure he'll calm down when he sees how cute these little guys are. How could anyone not be charmed by fire hydrants painted to look like some of Tranquillity's most prominent citizens dressed up in Santa suits?"

Dylan steered his truck around the last curve on the road leading into Tranquillity. He was tired, his muscles ached and his mood had improved little since leaving the ranger station. He hated it when people who had no previous hiking experience, decided to test themselves on the trails in the Davis Mountains. Fortunately, the two lost hikers had been found, and although they'd been scared half out of their minds from spending a night on the side of a mountain without shelter, neither had suffered serious injury during their ordeal.

His thoughts on the teenage boys he'd helped find earlier in the afternoon, it took a few seconds for his mind to register what his eyes were seeing. He stomped on the brake to bring his truck to a crawl and stared openmouthed as he slowly drove down Main Street. Instead of plain red fire hydrants, a short, squatty, brightly painted Santa Claus stood on every corner.

He swore a blue streak. They had to be the most ridiculous-looking things he'd ever seen. They even beat that cheap toupee old Corny insisted Myron wear to Luke's every Saturday night.

Pulling into his reserved parking space in front of the sheriff's office, Dylan paid little attention to the Santa hydrant standing guard in front of the building. In a rush to find out what was going on, his leg bumped into it as he walked past and he instinctively reached down to rub his knee. His fingers stuck slightly and when he glanced, first at his hand, then at the red paint on his jeans, he rattled off a word that would have gotten his mouth washed out with soap if his mother had been alive to hear him.

"Jason, what the hell happened out there?" he bellowed as he shoved open the office door.

Startled out of his nap, the wide-eyed young man almost fell off the chair he had tipped back against the wall behind the desk. Jumping to his feet, he placed his hand on his service revolver. "Where's the disturbance? Should I call the auxiliary for backup?"

"No, dammit," Dylan said impatiently. He jerked his thumb toward the street. "What happened out there today with the fire hydrants?"

Jason visibly relaxed. "Did you notice the likeness?" he asked, his grin wide.

"Likeness?"

"This is gonna be priceless," Jason said, laughing as he rounded the desk. He motioned for Dylan to follow him.

"Dammit, Jason, I'm not playing games," Dylan growled. But he followed his deputy outside.

Choking on his laughter, Jason pointed to the hydrant Dylan had run into only moments before. "Look like anybody you know?"

Dylan walked around to the front of the hydrant. There stood a two-foot miniature of himself in a Santa suit, complete with green eyes and a star painted on his chest, grinning back at him.

"The B.S. Club kicked off the first phase of their Main Street Project today," Jason said. He shook his head. "First time I ever remember them doing anything, besides sitting around and swapping the latest gossip."

Dylan's left eyebrow twitched rapidly and his stomach clenched into a painful knot at the mention of the B.S. Club. Brenna had been head of the committee responsible for the fire hydrants. When the women finally stopped talking and actually started doing something, everything suddenly got a lot more complicated than it had ever been in the past.

"Has Myron called yet?" he asked. Dylan could just imagine the conniption the mayor had gone into when he found out about the hydrants.

"Nope." Jason chuckled. "But he's the only council member who hasn't."

Dylan's stomach churned like a cement mixer as he walked back into the office. "I'll call Myron, while you call Ed and Luke. Tell them I want to see them here in the office first thing Monday morning. No excuses."

"Won't you see them tonight over at Luke's?" Jason asked as he picked up the phone. "You could set up the meeting then."

Dylan shook his head when he thought of all the complaints he'd be getting from the men. "I'm not going to Luke's this evening. I'm not in a very sociable mood."

Two hours later, standing on Brenna's newly repaired porch, Dylan felt as if the sun had risen on a new day when she opened the door. Her smile, the sparkle of happiness in her eyes, made his heart race. She was genuinely glad to see him.

Reaching for her, he pulled her into his arms. "Do you mind staying here instead of going to Luke's this evening?"

"No. I don't mind at all." She looked concerned. "Is everything all right?"

Not by a long shot. "Yeah," he lied, shrugging out of his leather jacket. "Everything's fine. I'm just a little tired, that's all."

"Me, too." She hung his jacket and Resistol on the coatrack, then turned to wind her arms around his neck. She gazed up at him with a satisfied smile. "I helped paint—"

Dylan immediately fused his lips to hers. He didn't need to be told what she'd been up to. He'd seen the fruits of her labor firsthand and wanted to avoid having to make a comment.

He kissed her thoroughly, then lifted his head to gaze down into her startled eyes. "I've missed you."

"Pete, I don't know if we should go to Luke's or not. Looks like there's going to be plenty of action right here tonight."

Dylan looked up to see Abigail's approving grin as she and Pete strolled into the room.

"Yeah, but it's gonna be *their* action, sugar." Pete kissed Abigail's cheek. "I want some of our own. Now, let's get goin'."

Dylan watched Abigail's cheeks turn pink. He'd bet she didn't blush very often. "Have a good time," he said, biting back a grin.

Abigail winked at him. "We'd wish you the same thing, but it's obvious you will."

"We're takin' your Chevy, Dylan," Pete said, hustling Abigail toward the door. "Since Brenna's car is back from the body shop, you've got hers if you change your mind about comin' over to the dance." When he passed Dylan, Pete lowered his voice. "We'll be back around midnight. But if we decide to come home earlier, I'll call first."

Dylan laughed. "I'd appreciate that, Uncle Pete."

When Pete and Abigail closed the door behind them, Dylan placed his arm around Brenna's shoulders and steered her toward the couch. "You don't mind staying here to watch a movie?"

She shook her head. "Actually, I'm rather glad. I'm pretty tired from helping the Beautification Society paint the fire hydrants today."

Dylan's eyebrow started to twitch as he sat down. He had a sinking feeling he knew what was coming next.

"By the way, did you notice them when you got back this afternoon?" she asked, settling herself beside him.

Well, there it was. The question he'd wanted to avoid as long as possible. He had a sneaking suspicion that if he told her what he really thought of them, she'd never speak to him again. But his conscience wouldn't allow him to lie to her either.

Uncomfortable with the whole situation, he cleared his throat. "Uh…yeah, I saw them when I drove through town."

"Well, what do you think?" she asked, smiling eagerly. "Aren't they unique?"

So's a longhorn steer, but I don't want one of them on Main Street, either.

"They're definitely different," he said evasively. He jumped to his feet. "Do you have some popcorn? We can't watch a movie without popcorn."

Clearly confused that he'd changed the subject so fast, Brenna nodded as she rose from the couch. "Sure. Why don't you come in and talk to me while I put it into the microwave?"

Happy to be off the hook for the moment, Dylan teased. "Are you sure it won't catch fire?"

She made a face at him as they entered the kitchen. "Unless the microwave malfunctions, you should be safe." Placing the bag inside, she set the timer. "You never did say what you thought of the fire hydrants."

Dylan felt the twitch over his left eye go completely berserk. He should've known better than to think Brenna would be content with the noncommittal answer he'd given her. And her hopeful expression made him feel like a heel. It would take a blind man or a fool not to see how enthusiastic she was over the damnable things.

He gave her a sideways glance. He couldn't bring himself to tell her he thought they were uglier than a day old vulture, so he hedged, "I hadn't given them much thought."

"How silly of me. Of course, you haven't. You were searching for those two boys lost up in the mountains." She made him feel worse when she gave him an understanding smile as she removed the popcorn from the microwave and emptied it into a bowl. "I heard they found them safe and sound this afternoon."

He nodded. "They were both scared spitless from being out there on the trail all night, and hungry as hell, but none the worse for wear."

"I'm sure that was frightening for you, too," she said, her voice filled with compassion. "Not knowing if you'd find them hurt, or worse, had to have given you several anxious moments."

His spirits sank lower. Her compassion made him feel like a low-down, double-dealing snake, even though he hadn't done anything wrong. But not wanting to tell her how ridiculous those hydrants looked made him feel as if he had—or was about to.

He had to move. The more understanding Brenna became, the worse he felt. Grabbing the bowl, he spun around and left the room. "Come on, we'll miss the beginning of the movie."

Brenna stared in stunned silence as Dylan made a hasty retreat. Something wasn't right, and she had every intention of finding out what it was.

"Dylan, what's going on?" she demanded, following him into the living room. "You've acted strange ever since I mentioned the fire hydrants."

When he turned to face her, she could have sworn he winced. But just as quickly as the expression appeared, it vanished. "What makes you think something's going on?"

She might have been slow to catch on, but she had a good idea what bothered him. "Your mood has nothing to do with being tired, or with finding those two lost teenagers, does it?" Walking up to him, she laid her hand on his arm. "Why don't you just come out and tell me you don't like the Santa Claus hydrants?"

He sank down on the couch, leaned his head back and closed his eyes. "I didn't want to hurt your feelings."

"Since when has the truth ever been more hurtful than a lie?" she asked, planting her hands on her hips. "Now, tell me what you really think of them."

She watched him open first one eye, then the other to peer up at her. Taking a deep breath, he cringed. "To tell you the truth, I think they're tacky as hell."

"Now, that didn't hurt, did it?" she asked, seating herself beside him on the couch.

"You're not upset?" He looked and sounded incredulous.

"No." She reached down and picked up a kernel of popcorn from the bowl he held, then placed it to his lips. "You'll get used to them. Besides, they won't be so out of place when the second phase of the project is completed."

He placed the bowl of popcorn on the end table, then rubbing at his left eyebrow, asked, "There's a second phase?"

Brenna nodded. "We plan on—"

But before she could tell him about the next step in the Beautification Society's plans to decorate for the Christmas season, Dylan pulled her onto his lap, brought his mouth down on hers and kissed her with a passion that took her breath away.

Her eyes drifted shut and Brenna felt as if the world spun out of control as Dylan slid his tongue across her lips, once, twice, then slipped between them to trace the inner recesses of her mouth. Playing a game of advance and retreat, he coaxed her into following his lead and when she slipped between his lips, to learn the taste of him, a feminine power she'd never felt before swept through her. All thoughts of Santa Claus fire hydrants, Main Street and the town of Tranquillity faded to nothingness when his groan of pleasure vibrated against her mouth.

Encouraged by his reaction, she tangled her hands in his thick hair as she lost herself in the moment. Sparkles of light danced behind her eyelids, but the thrill of kissing him once again was nothing compared to the feel of his hands on her body as he slid his palms beneath her sweater to stroke the sensitive skin across her rib cage. At the feel of his hard arousal against her bottom, shivers of excitement coursed through her and headed straight for the pit of her belly.

The feeling was so poignant that it startled her with its intensity and allowed a degree of sanity to intrude. ''Dylan, what are we—''

Pulling his hands from beneath her sweater, Dylan's chest rose and fell against hers as he took several deep breaths. ''Don't worry, darlin'.'' He placed her on the couch beside him, then handed her the bowl of popcorn. ''I meant it when I told you we'd take this one step at a time.''

"I think we just skipped step one and moved right on to step two," she said, feeling as if she'd run a marathon.

His deep, sexy chuckle sent a fresh wave of goose bumps skipping over her skin. Without a word, she handed him the bowl of popcorn, then reached into the candy dish on the coffee table for a handful of chocolate drops. Having chocolate was much safer than having Dylan, she told herself as she hastily unwrapped the silver foil and popped a piece of candy into her mouth.

Six

When the mayor and councilmen arrived Monday morning for the meeting he had requested, Dylan ushered them into his office and slammed the door. "Which one of you gave the B.S. Club permission to paint the fire hydrants?" he asked, motioning for the three men to seat themselves in the chairs in front of his desk.

"It sure wasn't me," Luke Washburn said emphatically, plopping down in one of the chairs.

Ed Taylor shook his head as he and Myron took their seats. "It wasn't me either."

When they all turned to stare at Myron, he remained strangely silent, and Dylan thought the man just might hang himself if he didn't stop fingering his bolo tie.

"Myron, do you have any idea who gave the B.S.

Club permission to do this?'' Dylan asked, already knowing the answer as he sank into the chair behind his desk.

The rotund little man's face turned beet-red. "Cornelia said it would be done in good taste and—''

"Good taste?'' Dylan and the other men shouted in unison.

Myron's shoulders sagged "—she threatened to stop cookin'.''

"Well, hell, Myron, you didn't have to let them vandalize the fire hydrants,'' Luke said, sounding as disgusted as he looked. "I run a restaurant. I could of fed you.''

Myron's expression conveyed his misery. "She said I'd have to sleep on the couch till I came to my senses, too.''

"I guess it would get mighty lonely sleepin' by yourself,'' Ed said, understanding written all over his face.

Myron snorted. "Aw, hell, Ed. I ain't worried about sleepin' by myself, or doin' without for a while. It's that damned couch that bothers me. There's a loose spring right in the middle of the blasted thing that pokes me in the butt every time I lay down.'' He rubbed his rump as if the thought of it caused pain. "I think she keeps it around just to threaten me when she wants her way.''

Dylan watched the exchange, then sighed heavily. "Giving them permission to paint the hydrants isn't the problem. What I'd like to know is whose bright idea it was to plaster my face on the one outside?''

"They painted every one of the danged things to resemble somebody,'' Luke Washburn complained.

"My wife, Helen, painted the one in front of our place and made me look like a damned Santa troll."

"Yeah, one that's been on a real bender," Ed chortled.

"If I were you, I wouldn't act too cocky, Taylor." Luke laughed. "Your wife painted yours with its eyes crossed."

"Isn't that the most pitiful-lookin' thing you ever saw?" Ed shook his head. "I told Emily she'd better buy herself a pair of specs or quit that damned paintin'. I know I ain't the best-lookin' man around, but I ain't *that* homely."

"Dylan, I don't know why you've got your shorts in a bunch," Luke said, turning back to face him. "Yours looks better than most."

"That's right," Ed chimed in. "At least that Montgomery gal can paint."

When Ed mentioned Brenna's involvement, Dylan's left eyebrow started twitching and his stomach felt as if little men in spiked shoes were doing an Irish jig in his belly. He didn't need the added complications of the B.S. Club project, on top of trying to deal with his feelings for Brenna.

"Dylan, you've been seein' that little gal pretty regular," Ed said thoughtfully.

"Yeah, and the women didn't get all fired-up about changin' the way things have always been until she came to town and started them danged classes," Luke groused.

"You gotta do somethin' about all this, Dylan," Ed said in earnest.

Dylan sat forward. "Now, hold it right there. It's *your* wives who came up with this hare-brained scheme. Besides, I can't, and won't, try to tell Brenna what to do, or not do. I'm not getting involved.''

''Oh, yes, you are,'' Myron said, jumping to his feet. He paced back and forth in front of Dylan's desk. ''You're gonna have to start snoopin' around more if we intend to stop this before they completely ruin the town.''

''That's right, Dylan,'' Ed added. ''Knowin' that bunch, if we don't stop 'em now, come this spring you'll be drivin' around in the sheriff's truck with pink and yellow daisies painted on the sides.''

''Since you ain't married, it won't cause you near the grief it could cause us,'' Luke said earnestly.

Dylan tasted defeat and it sat heavily on an already knotted stomach. ''What can *I* do? Brenna has a mind of her own. I can't tell her what to do, any more than you men can tell your wives.''

Myron looked thoughtful. ''We don't want you to tell her nothin', boy. Try askin' her what they have up their sleeves next. Then when you find out, let us know so we can head 'em off 'fore they do something else to make a mockery of Tranquillity.''

Ed Taylor stood up. ''Now that we've got that settled, I'm goin' by the drugstore to pick up a box of chocolates for Emily.''

''Why you doin' that?'' Luke asked.

''To make amends,'' Ed answered as he started for the door. ''Myron may not care about sleepin' all by his lonesome, but I do.''

''Me, too.'' Looking thoughtful, Luke followed him. ''I'm pretty sure Helen got offended when I told her the best thing she could do would be to throw them paints and brushes away and buy a dog to play with.''

''If you two are buyin' candy for your wives, I'd better buy some for Cornelia,'' Myron said, joining them. At their questioning look, he shrugged. ''I need some kind of insurance against that damned couch.''

Dylan watched the three men file out of his office. He was stuck between a rock and a hard place. No matter which way he turned, he couldn't win.

On one hand, he wholeheartedly agreed with the men. The women did have some cockamamie ideas. God only knew what they planned to do next.

But on the other hand, he couldn't forget the excitement in Brenna's eyes when she talked about her role in the B.S. Club's plans. She was genuinely thrilled to have been asked to join the women and become involved in the community so quickly. And he'd be damned before he did anything to take that happiness from her.

His gaze landed on the clock and he noticed it was already after lunch. He couldn't believe he'd wasted most of the morning listening to the council members' impotent complaints, then the rest of it trying to figure out what his own role was in the whole mess.

Shaking his head, Dylan made the decision to put it out of his mind. He had a feeling he could spend the rest of the day speculating on what he could do to resolve the matter and never come up with a solution. Besides, thinking about it just made his eyebrow twitch and his stomach churn.

Brenna shivered uncontrollably as she hurried down the sidewalk. Why had she opted to walk from her shop instead of driving the distance to the grade school? In the hour she'd been inside working with the fourth graders, the temperature had dropped a good twenty degrees and the cold rain pelting down on her felt like icy needles.

If only the storm had waited just a few more minutes, she'd have reached her shop before the downpour started. But it hadn't and instead of being dry and warm, she was completely soaked and chilled to the bone.

For the third time in as many minutes, she wondered what had possessed her to choose a Polynesian Christmas tale and a hula girl costume for today's story hour. The rain had quickly soaked the grass skirt, and besides clinging to her legs like pieces of limp spaghetti, it felt as if it weighed twenty pounds. She'd worn her hair down and the long, wet strands slapped her in the face with every gust of wind.

But if there was any part of her that felt more miserable than another, it had to be her feet. The flip-flop shoes she'd worn offered no protection from the weather at all. Her feet were drenched, extremely cold, and with every step the shoes slopped cold water up from the sidewalk onto the backs of her legs. Fortunately, she'd thought to throw a jacket in her tote bag and her hot-pink sports bra was blessedly dry. At least, for the moment.

Why hadn't she opted to wear mukluks and tell the story of *Nanook of the North?* she wondered as she plodded through yet another puddle. At least she'd be warmer than she was now.

Trying not to think about how miserable she was, it took a moment for her to realize that the sheriff's

SUV had pulled up beside her. When the power window slid down, Dylan was frowning. "Come on. Get in out of the rain."

Brenna was so glad to see him, she didn't think twice about accepting his offer, even though he'd told her to get into the truck instead of asking. Opening the door, she quickly slid into the passenger side of the nice, warm vehicle and closed the door.

"N-nice day…f-for ducks…w-wouldn't you say?" She shivered uncontrollably and her teeth chattered so badly they sounded like castanets.

"Damn, darlin', you're frozen," Dylan said, turning the heat to full blast. The warm air immediately washed over her and felt absolutely heavenly.

"Th-thank you…f-for the…r-ride," she managed to get out around her clicking teeth.

Shifting the SUV into park, he reached over to rub his hands up and down her arms. "Why didn't you drive to the school? Didn't you hear the weather report this morning about a blue norther blowing through?"

"I d-didn't listen to…t-the radio this morning. Besides, I th-thought I would be…finished before it started raining." The chattering began to slow down as she felt the heat from Dylan's hands flow through her. "I was wrong."

"Obviously." He reached over to help her out of her wet jacket, then slipped out of his dry, leather one and placed it around her shoulders.

His gaze leisurely traveled the length of her, stopping at her sports bra, then traveling down to her skirt. The wet strands of grass had parted so her thighs were mostly exposed. Her cheeks heated and, reaching down, she tried to arrange the strips to cover herself.

"I'm afraid this isn't very appropriate for this type of weather," she said, uncertain whether the shiver that snaked up her spine was due to the weather, or from his heated gaze.

His deep chuckle sent a fresh wave of goose bumps sweeping across her skin and she knew the tremor had nothing to do with the chilling rain. "I can honestly say this is the first Story Lady costume you've worn that I approve of," he said, his smile sending another shiver coursing though her. His smile turning serious, he asked, "Do you have another change of clothes at the shop?"

"No, but I have some in my tote bag." She pulled a soggy turtleneck sweater and a pair of equally wet jeans from the canvas tote. "Well, they were dry a few minutes ago."

"I'll take you by your place first, then drive you to your shop."

Shifting the truck back into drive, Dylan remained silent as he drove Brenna to her house. He hated that she'd gotten cold and wet, but appreciated the hell out of the fact that the rain had provided him with more than a fair view of her luscious body.

Her bright pink spandex sports top did little to conceal that her nipples had peaked from the cold, and the droplets of water from her wet hair sliding down into the garment had caused his mouth to go dry. But when he'd noticed the grass skirt had parted, revealing her smooth thighs, his body had hardened so fast that it had momentarily made him dizzy.

"It looks like Pete and your grandmother have

plans for the afternoon,'' he said, pointing to his antique Chevy truck pulling from Brenna's driveway. He watched Pete and Abigail wave as they drove past. "I wonder where they're headed this time?"

"Granny mentioned something about her and Pete spending the afternoon and most of the evening down in Alpine," Brenna said, rummaging around in the depths of her tote. "By the way, would you like to come over to watch a movie after dinner?"

"Sure. What time should I come by?"

"I have a meeting right after I close the shop, but I should be finished by seven," she added, dragging several items out of the canvas bag. She sighed heavily. "Well, that's just great. I must have left my house keys on the dresser this morning and I have no way of getting into the house to change."

"You don't have an extra key under the doormat or hidden in a flowerpot somewhere?" he asked, turning the SUV into the drive.

She shook her head. "Granny says that's the first place a burglar would look."

"I agree," he said, nodding. "But most people do it anyway. I advise having an extra key made and carrying it in your purse or wallet." He left the motor running as they sat staring out the windshield at the house. "I don't suppose you have an extra key at the shop?"

She worried her lower lip as she shook her head. "Afraid not."

He picked up the microphone to radio Jason that he wouldn't be back to the office until later, then backed the truck out onto the street. "Looks like I'll have to take you to my place."

"We can't go to your house," she protested. "I need to reopen my shop for the rest of the afternoon."

He continued to drive toward the cabin he shared with Pete on the outskirts of town. "I doubt you'll have that much business in this kind of weather, but after I loan you a pair of sweats, I'll bring you back to town."

The thought of her wearing his clothes sent his blood pressure soaring and made him harder than hell. If just thinking about her in his baggy sweatsuit aroused him this much, he was in bigger trouble than he'd ever imagined possible.

Steering the truck up the lane to his cabin, Dylan tried not to dwell on the fact that very soon he'd be inside his home with Brenna. Alone. And she'd be taking off her clothes and putting on his. Sweat popped out on his upper lip and he had to concentrate to keep from groaning out loud.

"I hope Granny and Pete make it to Alpine safely," Brenna said, bringing him back to the present.

"I'm sure they will." He pulled the SUV to a stop beside the front porch of his home. "Pete's seen more than his share of blue northers move through." Dylan opened the driver's door, then came around to help her from the passenger side. "Just be glad that this far south we get rain and not snow. It's my bet the Panhandle is knee-deep in it about now."

"It feels cold enough to snow," she said, shivering visibly.

"It's chilly and you're wet. It just seems colder than it really is." He placed his hands at her waist to lift her down from the truck and gritted his teeth at the feel of her satiny skin against his rough palms.

Her eyes met his and he could tell that she was gripped by the same tension he was. He quickly stepped back and waited for her to precede him up the porch steps.

Maybe this hadn't been such a good idea. He was trying his damnedest to be a gentleman, but it seemed everything was working against him. He was going to be alone with Brenna in his cabin, she had on an outfit that sent his temperature soaring and he was harder than he'd been in a month of Sundays. It was a lethal combination to his good intentions any way he looked at it, and not at all encouraging.

When he opened the door and they stepped inside the darker interior, he reached out to turn on a lamp and cursed vehemently. "It looks like the storm has knocked out the power. Stay here and I'll be right back."

Entering the kitchen area, he removed a kerosene lamp from one of the shelves in the pantry, lit the wick, then went back into the living room where Brenna stood looking cold, wet and more desirable than any woman he'd ever seen. "Let's get you something warm and dry to put on," he said, placing the lamp on the mantel over the fireplace.

He went into his bedroom to find her something to wear, but made it a point not to look at his king-size bed. No telling how many different scenarios his suddenly active imagination would conjure up.

A sudden flash of light and a deafening clap of thunder preceded a startled cry from the other room.

The hair on the back of his neck stood straight up and every nerve in his body came to full alert.

"Are you all right?" he asked, rushing back to where Brenna stood, staring out the picture window.

As she nodded, she pointed toward the lane. "I was startled when lightning struck that tree."

"This can't be happening," he muttered, his hand tightening into a fist around the sweatsuit and thick socks he'd retrieved from the dresser.

Looking at the smoldering tree stump, then at the live oak blocking the drive, he couldn't believe how fate had stepped in to make matters worse. They were trapped, and there was no way they'd be making it back to town until the storm moved on and he could use the chain saw to clear the lane. And, if the reports were accurate, that wouldn't be until sometime tomorrow afternoon.

Dylan swallowed hard. He and Brenna would have to spend the night in his cabin. Alone.

Sweat popped out on his forehead and his groin tightened predictably. Glancing down at his chest, he almost groaned. The star pinned to his shirt represented justice, integrity and honor—principles he'd tried his damnedest to uphold all of his life. But at the moment, he wasn't sure he'd be able to live up to the last part of the code.

He glanced down at the woman standing beside him. With each passing second, his thoughts were becoming increasingly less honorable and exceedingly more lusty.

Suddenly unable to stand still, he handed her the sweats and the thick socks, then turned to the fireplace. "Get changed and I'll see about getting a fire started." Without looking at her, he gritted his teeth and added, "We're going to be here a while."

"Is there something I can do to help?" Brenna asked, watching Dylan place logs in the stone fireplace.

He shook his head. "There's not much to do. We'll just have to sit tight and make the best of things until the storm lets up."

She pushed up the sleeves of the oversize gray sweatshirt and reached for her tote bag. Please let there be something chocolate somewhere inside, she prayed. But the only thing she found that was even remotely related to her chocolate addiction was a crumpled wrapper and a coupon for fifty cents off her next candy purchase.

Sighing, Brenna put the canvas bag back on the cushion beside her and stared at Dylan's broad back. They were trapped in his cozy cabin and there wasn't any way out until it stopped raining.

She glanced out the window. It didn't appear that would happen any time soon.

"In case you're wondering," he said, sounding calm, "we're probably going to be spending the night here."

Turning back to face him, she nodded. "I figured that would be the case."

How had she managed to sound so matter-of-fact when her insides fluttered wildly and her pulse beat like a little miniature snare drum?

She knew she was grasping at straws, but she had to ask, "You couldn't use the Explorer to pull the tree out of the way enough to drive past it?"

He shook his head. "Afraid not." His back to her, he continued to work at starting the fire. "And I can't saw the tree up and move it until the storm lets up." He chuckled. "I'm not real big on dodging lightning bolts at any time, but especially not when I'm holding a chainsaw with a twenty-inch steel bar."

"No, that wouldn't be a very good idea," she agreed, glancing back at the fallen tree. "I suppose I should call and cancel my meeting for this afternoon." She hated the fact that it would put the Beautification Society behind on their plans. Knowing she had no choice, she retrieved her planner from the tote. "Do you think your phone still works?"

Dylan rose to his feet and walked over to a desk in the corner of the room. Picking up the receiver, he listened, then set it back on its base. "It's out, too."

"How am I going to let the ladies on the Main Street committee know that I won't be able to meet with them?"

"I'll go out and use the radio in the cruiser to contact Jason. I need to let him know what's happened anyway. While I'm at it, I'll have him make the calls for you." Dylan started toward the door, then turned back. "Do you have a list of the members involved?"

She pulled a paper from her datebook, then handed it to him. "Please ask him to let everyone know we'll reschedule the meeting for next week. Do you think he would mind calling my house to leave a message for Granny and Pete, as well?"

"No problem," he said, walking to the door.

While Dylan went out to make the radio call to his deputy, Brenna curled up on the couch and stared at the blazing logs in the fireplace. When she left for the grade school just after lunch all she'd had on her mind was being the Story Lady for an hour, meeting with the Main Street committee to discuss the next phase to be completed before the Jamboree on Christmas Eve night, and asking Dylan if he'd like to come over for a movie. Now, she was having to cancel her meeting and planning to spend the night with him.

She shook her head. She wasn't spending the night *with* him. She was spending the night in his cabin and he just happened to be there with her.

She took a deep breath. Dylan's masculine scent on the clothes he'd loaned her assailed her senses and a tremor raced the length of her spine. She closed her eyes against the coil tightening in her lower belly. She'd tried to tell herself for days that she was spending time with him because it was preferable to spending time alone while her grandmother was out with Pete. But the truth was, no matter how hard she'd tried, she was falling head over heels for him. And it scared her silly.

Dylan cursed as he hung the mike back on the dashboard of the Explorer. He had the urge to punch something.

While he'd been giving Jason instructions about calling Brenna's place and the women on her planning committee, Myron had walked into the office. The man had been so excited about the fact that Brenna was having to cancel the meeting, Myron had told Dylan he intended to see that Dylan received a commendation for going above and beyond the call of duty in his effort to stop the B.S. Club.

Dylan had tried to explain that it was a bizarre act

of nature and that he had nothing to do with it, but Myron wasn't listening. All the man could concentrate on was the fact that future plans for the Main Street Project had been put on hold for a week, giving the men extra time to come up with a scheme to stop whatever the women had planned next.

Sighing heavily, Dylan got out of the truck and made a mad dash for the front porch. He was sick of hearing about the B.S. Club, the Main Street Project, and the men's desire to stop the women from making any further changes.

He stood with his hand on the doorknob. The way he saw it, he had a choice to make. He could either spend the rest of the day feeling guilty about his part in the men's attempt to stop the women of Tranquillity, or he could forget about the town and concentrate on enjoying Brenna's company.

For the first time in the past hour, he smiled. As far as he was concerned there was no contest. Myron, the B.S. Club and the Main Street Project be damned.

He was going to spend the rest of the day, and night, concentrating on the most exciting, desirable woman he'd ever met.

Seven

"**W**ould you like another s'more?" Dylan asked, pulling a long-handled barbecue fork with toasted marshmallows on it from the fireplace.

Sitting on the braided rug in front of the hearth, Brenna shook her head as she licked the sticky remnants of chocolate and marshmallow from her fingertips. His mouth suddenly felt as if it had been coated with cotton. But when her little pink tongue darted out to remove a graham cracker crumb from her index finger, sweat popped out on his forehead and upper lip.

"No, thank you," she said, smiling. "I've had my chocolate fix. I'll be fine for a while."

"I'm glad I found Pete's stash of candy bars," Dylan teased, in an attempt to keep things light. "I'd hate for you to go into chocolate withdrawal."

"Oh, that wouldn't be pretty," she said, shaking her head. She grinned impishly. "You should have seen me the day we painted the fire hydrants. I'd gone all day without something chocolate and by late afternoon, I was not someone you'd want to be around."

At the mention of the Main Street Project, Dylan felt his eyebrow begin to twitch rhythmically. If he never heard another word about the B.S. Club and their plans it would be all too soon.

"When we start on—"

He quickly broke off a small section of chocolate and placed it to her lips, effectively cutting off what she was about to say. "I don't want you getting cranky," he said, hoping his smile looked less forced than it felt. "And I don't want to discuss anything about the Main Street Project."

"Why not?" Her throaty laughter as she chewed the candy sent a shaft of longing straight through him. "We have the cutest Christmas—"

"I'd rather concentrate on you," he interrupted. He reached out to run his index finger along her soft cheek. "You're much more exciting."

Dylan watched her luminous blue eyes widen a moment before she broke off another piece of the candy bar and popped it into her mouth.

"You know what they say about chocolate, don't you?" he asked, breaking off another piece.

She shook her head.

"Studies have shown that eating chocolate creates the same chemical reaction in the brain that making love does," he said, reaching down to lace his fingers with hers.

"I think I've heard that, too," she said, her gaze reflecting the same awareness he felt.

The feel of her smooth skin and the sound of her sultry voice did strange things to his insides and sent his temperature soaring. When she glanced up at him from beneath her lashes, desire—urgent and hot—flowed through his veins.

The shadows cast by the kerosene lamp and the logs blazing in the fireplace lent an intimacy to the room that stole his breath. Bathed in the soft glow, she was the most beautiful woman he'd ever seen, and he wanted her more than he'd ever wanted anything in his life.

He tugged her forward. "Come here, darlin'."

"I doubt this is wise," Brenna said, her gaze locking with his as he pulled her onto his lap. She knew she should put up more than a token protest, considering their situation. But the truth was, she wanted Dylan to hold her, to once again make her feel cherished and desirable.

"It probably isn't wise," he agreed. He placed a piece of chocolate between his lips, then brushed it across hers. Kissing her, he gently pushed the candy into her mouth with his tongue, then drawing back, he smiled at her. "But what the hell. I've never been accused of being the sharpest knife in the drawer."

She closed her eyes as the rich taste of chocolate spread across her taste buds. "Dylan?"

His mouth touched hers again in a feathery caress as he licked the chocolate from her lips. "What?"

"Please kiss me." His tantalizing caresses weren't nearly enough.

A groan rumbled up from deep in his chest and he

pulled her close, but continued to tease her. "In a minute, darlin'," he whispered against her lips. "This heightens the anticipation."

She shook her head and put her arms around his shoulders to tangle her fingers in his thick, black hair. "No, it doesn't." She suddenly felt quite breathless. "It just makes me crazy."

He chuckled and the low sexy sound caused her heart to skip several beats and the butterflies in the pit of her stomach to flap wildly. She knew she was playing with fire. They were completely alone, with no chance of interruptions. But she didn't care. She wanted Dylan to kiss her. And more.

The thought should have sent her running as fast as her feet would carry her back to the safety of her shop in Tranquillity. But the fear of being intimate with Dylan, of holding his body to hers, and experiencing the contrast of a man and woman for the first time didn't frighten her nearly as much as the thought of never knowing the power of his love.

He barely touched her mouth with his, then gently sucked on her lower lip. "I want you to remember this kiss for the rest of your life, Brenna."

She would have told him there was no way she could ever forget it, but his tongue slipped inside to trace her teeth, then stroke the inner recesses, and Brenna lost the ability to think of anything but the man holding her so tightly against him. The hunger of his kisses, the taste of his passion, sent heat surging through her veins and made every cell in her body tingle to life.

"You taste like chocolate and sweet, sexy woman," he said, his low drawl sending quivers of delight shimmering through her. Her nipples tightened and she arched against him in an effort to get closer.

The hard muscles of his chest crushed her breasts as he lifted her, then stretched them both out on the rug in front of the hearth. Melting against him, she reveled in the rapid beating of his heart, his groan of pleasure when she traced his nape with her fingertips.

Brenna brought her hands down to his shoulders, then giving him a little push to create a space between them, she worked on the snaps of his chambray shirt. She wanted to feel the warmth of his skin, the steely muscles that she'd admired the first day they met.

"I want to touch you," she murmured.

Her heart stopped, then took off at a gallop. She couldn't believe the degree of passion in her tone, or that she'd spoken her thoughts aloud.

But before she had time to dwell on the admission, Dylan rose to his knees, yanked the snap closures of his shirt free and quickly shrugged out of the garment. Her breath caught at the sight of his well-developed chest and stomach. The man could pose for a calendar and easily sell a million copies, she decided as she reached up to trace the ridges of sinew with her fingertips. His sharp intake of breath encouraged her and she placed her palms over his pectoral muscles to feel his flat male nipples pucker in response.

"We're going to touch each other," he promised.

His dark green eyes held her captive as he took her hands in his. Pulling her to a kneeling position in front of him, he slipped his hands beneath the hem of the sweatshirt he'd loaned her to stroke the sensitive skin from her waist to the underside of her breasts.

The raw desire she saw in his heated gaze, the feel of his callused palms on her skin and the clean, manly scent of him, created a longing in her that she'd never known. It was as if he'd unlocked her heart, her soul. She wanted to make love with him, to have him become a part of her body as she would be part of his.

In that moment, she knew beyond a shadow of doubt that she was falling in love with Dylan. But before she had time to think of the implications of her discovery, Dylan eased his hands up to cup her bare breasts.

"You aren't wearing a bra," he said, smiling as he supported the weight of her with his palms.

"It was too wet from the rain," she said, her cheeks heating as she tried to explain why she wasn't fully dressed.

The smoldering look he gave her took her breath. "I'm glad." Leaning forward, he kissed her. "I want to see you, darlin'."

Unable to make her voice work, she nodded without hesitation.

He must have sensed her vulnerability because he gave her an encouraging smile a moment before he swept his hands upward and stripped her of the sweatshirt. When he tossed it aside, her first inclination was to cover herself. But she heard his sharp intake of breath, saw the spark in his eyes turn to flames of desire, and any lingering inhibitions she might have had melted away.

Smiling appreciatively, he took her hands in his

and placed them on his chest before cupping her breasts with his palms. "You're beautiful, Brenna."

He gently chafed the beaded tips with the pads of his thumbs, then leaning forward to kiss the hollow behind her ear, whispered, "I'm going to taste you."

As he nibbled his way down her neck to her shoulder, then her collarbone, her head fell back and she trembled at the feel of his lips on her skin. Delicious, honeyed heat flowed through her to form a heavy coil of need in her nether regions and she had to bite her lower lip to keep from moaning aloud. But when his hot mouth closed around her taught nipple and his tongue flicked over her tight flesh, she couldn't have stopped the sound from escaping if her life depended on it.

Dylan lifted his head. He didn't think he'd ever heard a sweeter sound than that of the pleasure he'd created in Brenna. "That's it, darlin'. Let me hear you. Let me know how I make you feel and what you need."

Rising to his feet he pulled her up with him, then placed his hands at her waist to dip his fingers beneath the elastic band of the sweatpants he'd loaned her. The discovery that she wasn't wearing panties sent a shockwave of heat straight to his groin and his straining body felt as if it just might bust the zipper of his fly.

"They were wet, too," she said, unable to meet his gaze.

He put his finger under her chin and tilted her head up so their gazes met. "Do you have any idea how arousing it is for me just knowing you were naked inside my clothes?" When she shook her head, he cupped her bottom and pulled her lower body to him. "Does this give you an idea?"

Her eyes widened at the feel of his arousal pressed to her lower belly and he watched with mounting satisfaction as the spark of awareness in her eyes changed to a smoldering ember of passion. Determined to fan the spark into the flame of unbridled desire, Dylan stepped back, then slowly, carefully moved his hands downward. The too-big pants fell away from her hips and legs to land in a heap at her feet.

Air seemed in short supply as he looked at her. Brenna was shaped the way a woman should be, with full breasts, soft curves and nicely rounded hips. She wasn't the fragile type that a man was afraid to love for fear of breaking something when he held her to him. No, Brenna was a woman who could hold a man captive in her softness as she drained him of every last ounce of strength he possessed.

At first, she looked a bit unsure as she kicked free of the gray pool of fleece. But when her eyes met his, Dylan forgot all about her hesitant expression. Desire, passion and need were reflected in her blue gaze, and his only thought centered around removing the rest of his clothes and feeling all of her delicious body next to his.

With a practiced twist of his fingers, he worked the button at his waistband through the opening, eased the zipper down over his insistent arousal, then quickly shucked his jeans and briefs. Reaching for her, he wrapped her in his arms and pulled her to him.

The feel of her satiny skin finally touching his hair-roughened flesh, the sweet, womanly scent that was uniquely Brenna enveloping him, and the sound of her soft sigh as she melted against him sent his blood pressure into stroke range and his heartrate into overdrive. Taking several deep breaths to slow his runaway libido, he buried his face in the red-gold cloud of her hair. He'd never in his entire life been as turned on as he was at that very moment.

Unsure of how much more of the sweet torture his body could withstand, Dylan swung her up into his arms and headed for his bedroom. He wanted to take things slowly, to make love to Brenna the way she was meant to be loved—slowly, thoroughly.

When he reached the side of the king-size bed, he threw back the comforter, lowered her to the pristine sheets, and stretched out beside her. Pulling her into his arms, he kissed her again with every emotion he felt, but wasn't ready to identify.

By the time he broke the kiss, Dylan felt as if he might go up in flames. Never had desire been so intense, or his need for a woman so strong.

"Dylan, there's something I need to tell you," she said, her lips skimming his shoulder and sending a shock wave of heat to every part of him.

"What's that, honey?" he asked.

He propped his elbow on the mattress and rested his head on his hand. Staring down at the most beautiful woman he'd ever known, he lightly traced his index finger between the valley of her breasts, down her abdomen to her navel. Rewarded by her soft sigh and the trembling of her body at his touch, he continued his exploration. But when he reached the nest of curls at the juncture of her thighs, her body stiffened.

"You wanted to tell me something?" he asked, slowing his exploration in order to give her time to relax.

The uncertain look she'd worn earlier returned and gazing up at him, she worried her lower lip a moment before she nodded. "I've…never done this before."

She made the announcement so softly, he wasn't sure he'd heard correctly. "You've never been with a man?" The vulnerable look in her guileless blue eyes when she shook her head, touched something deep inside of him. "Not even the jerk who duped you into thinking the two of you would get married after he got out of law school?"

"We…" She stopped and shook her head again. "*I* never felt ready."

Dylan's heart stuttered. "And you feel ready now? With me?"

"Yes."

The firmness he detected in her voice, the sincerity in her gaze, shook him to the very foundation of his soul. Brenna hadn't given herself to the man she'd thought to eventually marry because it hadn't felt right. But she was ready to give herself to him.

An admission like Brenna had just made should have doused all traces of his desire and sent him running like a tail-tucked coyote. But the thought that she felt ready to make love with him when she'd never felt ready to share herself with any other man made Dylan's heart swell and his body throb with an intensity that caused his head to swim. Unable to express the depth of his feelings with words, he gathered her in his arms and kissed her with a passion that he'd never believed himself capable of.

As Dylan's mouth moved over hers, the apprehension that had built inside Brenna melted away and was quickly replaced with the sweet tension of renewed desire. His tongue plunged between her lips to explore her inner recesses and a kaleidoscope of shimmering light danced behind her closed eyes. His tongue teased hers and an empty ache began to pool in all of her secret places.

When he slid his hand back down her body to touch her intimately, every muscle in her body strained to be closer to him. He must have sensed her need, and parting her, he teased the tiny nub of her femininity with gentle, easy movements that heightened her excitement more than she'd ever dreamed possible. She'd never before experienced the intense sensations coursing through her, but when he dipped his finger inside her dewy moisture to stroke her, Brenna felt as if something inside her ignited and she was sure she would go up in flames.

Moaning her pleasure, she writhed against him as ribbons of desire twined into a deep coil of need in the pit of her stomach. "Please, Dylan—"

"Feel good?" he asked, his lips leisurely moving over her shoulder.

"Y-yes."

Raising his head, his expression took her breath. "Brenna, I want you more than I've ever wanted any woman in my life and I need to be inside you. Are you ready for that?"

"Yes."

"Are you sure?" he asked as he continued to

heighten her passion by moving his finger within her. "I'll do everything in my power not to hurt you, but this first time might not be as good for you as I'd like."

She'd accepted the fact that there would be a certain amount of discomfort her first time with a man, but Dylan's words chased away any hesitation she might have harbored. "I've never been more sure of anything in my life. Please, make love to me, Dylan."

A groan rumbled up from deep in his chest, then kissing her briefly, he reached inside the drawer of the bedside table to remove a small foil packet. As she watched him arrange their protection, a tiny sliver of doubt returned to invade the sensual haze surrounding her. She'd never seen a man's lower body other than in anatomy textbooks in college, but something told her that Dylan wasn't a small man.

When she glanced up, he was watching her. "Your body was made to hold a man's like you're about to hold mine, darlin'." He moved to gather her into his arms. "Just relax. We're going to fit together just fine."

His gentle kiss erased her uncertainty a moment before he parted her legs and moved over her. Holding her captive with his passionate gaze, he reached for her hand and together they guided him to her moist heat.

Brenna tensed involuntarily when she felt her body begin to stretch to accommodate his entry. But the mixture of tenderness and hungry desire in Dylan's eyes, his gentle words of encouragement as he drew back, then carefully pressed forward, reassured her. His body continued the rhythmic movements and with each slow, forward thrust she felt him slide more deeply inside her.

He soon met the resistance within her and she braced herself for the discomfort she knew would soon follow. But his steady gaze told her without words that everything would be all right a moment before he hugged her to him, covered her mouth with his, then pushed past the veil and completely sank himself inside her. Her breath caught momentarily at the shock of holding all of him, but he remained perfectly still and the discomfort quickly subsided.

She felt his taught muscles quiver when he propped himself on his forearms to gaze down at her and she could tell he was giving her time to adjust to his size and strength. "You're so tight. I don't want to hurt you. But I don't think I can stand much more of this, darlin'."

His face reflected the toll of his restraint and in that moment, Brenna knew she loved him with all of her heart and soul. Reaching up to touch his lean cheek, she whispered, "Please make love to me, Dylan."

With a growl of satisfaction, he leaned forward to kiss the sensitive hollow of her throat at the same time he drew his hips back. Easing forward, he repeated the movement again and again, setting a slow steady pace. Very soon his movements renewed her passion and the coil inside her tightened to unbearable proportions. She sensed that she was on the verge of an awakening, a liberation from the tension gripping her as she moved in time with Dylan, but unsure of what was to come, she tensed.

Apparently sensing her readiness, as well as her confusion, he held her close. "Just let go, darlin'," he said, his voice rough with passion. "I'll take care of you."

Trusting Dylan as she'd never trusted anyone, Brenna gave in to the increased rhythm of his love-making and was immediately consumed by wave after wave of pleasure washing through her. A moment later, groaning her name, he thrust into her one final time, and she felt him join her in the realm of soul-shattering release.

When the last spasms of his climax subsided and his heartrate slowly returned to normal, Dylan moved to Brenna's side and pulled her to him. Nothing in his past could compare to making love with the woman he held. He felt as if he'd died and gone to heaven.

"Are you all right, darlin'?" he asked, kissing the top of her head.

Snuggling against his chest, she nodded. "That was the most beautiful experience of my life."

"I didn't hurt you, did I?" He didn't think it had been overly uncomfortable for her, but he needed to know.

"No." She leaned back in his arms to gaze up at him. "Thank you for making my first time wonderful, Dylan."

Her first time. The knowledge that she'd waited for him to be the first man she was intimate with made his chest swell and his gut burn with the need to be the last. The thought of Brenna in another man's arms, sharing her body as she'd shared it with him, sent a shaft of deep need coursing through him to once again make her his.

Turning her to her back, Dylan kissed her closed eyes, the tip of her nose and her stubborn little chin. "I want you again, Brenna."

Opening her eyes, her smile warmed him to the very depths of his being. "I want you, too."

"Are you sure?" he asked, concerned that making love again so soon might cause her more discomfort.

Nodding her head, she brought her arms up to encircle his shoulders. "I've never been more sure of anything in my life. Make love to me again, Dylan."

Eight

The next afternoon, after Dylan had dealt with the tree blocking the lane, he drove Brenna home. But instead of finding his antique truck parked in her drive, as he expected, there was no sign of the vintage Chevy. "I wonder where Pete is?"

"I don't know, but I'm sure Granny's with him wherever he is," Brenna said, laughing.

Her sweet smile, the light of having been well-loved in her pretty blue eyes, caused a tightness in his chest and had his body reacting in a very predictable way. Damned if the woman couldn't make him hard by doing nothing more than looking at him.

Leaning over, he gave her a quick kiss, then opened the driver's door. "Remind me to thank your grandmother for keeping Pete occupied."

When he rounded the front of the Explorer to help

her from the truck, she smiled. "I think I should be the one thanking Pete for keeping Granny busy. You have no idea how challenging she can be at times."

Taking her hand in his, Dylan walked to the door with Brenna. "Looks like they're gone again," he said, removing a piece of paper taped to the inside of the storm door. Scanning the contents of the note, he frowned. "Good advice, but I don't know why they would bother taping it to the door."

"Let me see." She took the paper from him, then read it aloud. "The real key to safety is watching what's under your feet. Step carefully kids." Laughing, she shook her head. "My keys are under the step."

"How do you know?" he asked, completely confused.

She bent down to reach beneath the wooden step, then straightening, held up a set of keys in a small plastic bag. "It's a game we used to play when I was a child," she said, fitting the key into the deadbolt on the door. "Pick out every third word."

Following her into the house, he stood, reading the note while she walked into the kitchen. "Key...is... under...step. Well, I'll be damned. You two have a very effective way of communicating without anyone knowing what the hell you're talking about."

"Dylan—"

Something in her tone made him glance up. Brenna stood in the doorway, her complexion a ghostly pale. Rushing over to her, he demanded, "What's wrong?"

"I don't believe it." Her hand trembled as she

handed him another piece of paper. "They've used your truck to elope to Las Vegas."

"They've done what?" Surely he hadn't heard her right.

Dylan read the note, then shook his head. He thought it was great that his uncle Pete and Abigail had found happiness together in their golden years, but he wasn't nearly so enthusiastic about them taking his vintage truck as their get-away vehicle. He unthinkingly uttered a word that, if his father had been alive, would have tanned his hide for saying in front of a lady.

"Sorry," he muttered.

Apparently, Brenna was still too shocked to notice his less-than-polite language. "I can't believe this is happening," she said. She walked over to sink down on the couch. "Granny is actually getting married and I'm not going to be there to see it."

"Oh, yes you are, darlin'," he said, making a snap decision. He pulled her into his arms. "We're going to follow them."

She brightened. "We are?"

"Yep. You'll get to see your grandmother get married, and I'll get my truck back."

"But they've gotten almost a full day's head start on us." She sounded doubtful.

"That's true," he admitted. "But if I know Pete, they'll stop for the night in Albuquerque. He has a friend up that way and I'm betting they stay there tonight." Dylan checked his watch. "If we take off within the next hour, we should catch up to them by midnight."

"I left my car at the shop yesterday, but we could go by and get it for the trip," Brenna offered.

Dylan nodded. "We'll have to. I can't take the Explorer for a personal trip." He gave her a quick kiss, then set her away from him before he delayed their departure by taking her into the bedroom to make love to her for the rest of the day and night. "Now, go throw some things in a bag while I call Jason and fill him in on what's going on."

Once she'd trotted down the hall toward her bedroom, Dylan took a deep breath and dialed the sheriff's office. He wasn't happy that Pete had taken his truck. That antique Chevy was his pride and joy, and about the only thing Dylan had left that belonged to his father.

But he'd have to thank his uncle when they caught up to the elderly duo. By choosing to elope, Pete had handed Dylan the perfect excuse for spending more uninterrupted time with the most alluring woman he'd ever known as they drove the distance to Las Vegas.

"Granny, I still can't understand why you couldn't have gotten married back in Tranquillity," Brenna said as she closed the door to the honeymoon suite behind them.

Tired from the long trip, she yawned as she and her grandmother walked down the long hall to the elevator. She and Dylan had caught up with the geriatric duo in Albuquerque late last night, just as he had predicted. Then, rising early to drive the rest of the distance to Las Vegas, they'd spent what was left of the afternoon shopping for something to wear to Pete and Abigail's evening wedding.

"We chose Las Vegas because we wanted some-one out of the ordinary to marry us," Abigail said as they stepped onto the elevator. Straightening her cream-colored suit, her eyes twinkled merrily. "Can you think of a more radical way of getting married than having the King of Rock and Roll officiate the ceremony?"

Before Brenna could tell her grandmother that it was indeed unusual, the elevator doors swished open and there stood Dylan and Pete. Her pulse quickened and her breath caught. She hadn't seen him since their shopping trip that afternoon when Abigail insisted that she and Brenna use the honeymoon suite to dress for the wedding, while Dylan and Pete changed in the room that Dylan had checked into.

She smoothed a nervous hand down the skirt of the dark green, midlength dress her grandmother had cho-sen for her as she watched Dylan walk toward her. She'd never seen him look more handsome in the dark blue western-cut sports jacket, powder blue shirt and black jeans he'd bought for the honor of being best man.

"Dylan is one hot dude, isn't he?" her grand-mother whispered.

"He sure is," Brenna agreed before she could stop herself.

"You know, we could make this a double cere-mony," Abigail suggested.

"Granny, don't start," Brenna warned. But a warmth filled her at the thought of marrying Dylan.

"Ain't those two the prettiest gals you've ever seen?" she heard Pete ask Dylan. Stepping forward, Pete tucked Abigail's hand in the crook of his arm.

"Ready to get hitched up all good and proper, sugar?"

"I sure am, you old goat," Abigail answered, her smile absolutely radiant.

Dylan's gaze held Brenna's captive as he stepped forward to take her hands in his. The appreciation in his brilliant green eyes sent heat coursing through her veins and caused her toes to curl inside her new pumps.

Bringing her hands to his lips, he brushed a kiss on her sensitive skin. "You look beautiful, darlin'."

"Thank you," she said, hoping she didn't sound as breathless as she felt.

Before she could tell Dylan how good he looked, Pete cleared his throat. "Are you two gonna stand there lollygagin' over one 'nother, or you goin' with us?"

Dylan never took his eyes from hers and she felt as if she might drown in their depths as he tucked her to his side. "Lead the way, Uncle Pete. We're right behind you."

An hour later, Dylan helped Brenna from the back of the limousine in front of the hotel. He couldn't believe how fast the wedding had taken place. They'd no sooner walked into the chapel that Pete and Abigail had chosen to exchange their vows, than an Elvis impersonator gyrated his way to the altar, asked the two seniors if they promised to "love each other tender" for the rest of their lives, then pronounced them man and wife.

"We want you two to come up to our suite for a

toast,'' Abigail said as they all entered the hotel lobby.

Pete nodded. ''We have a couple of things we need to talk about with you kids.''

''Of course, we'll come up to your suite,'' Brenna said. She turned to Dylan. ''As best man, you should be the one doing the honors.''

Glancing at her, Dylan felt his lower body tighten. He'd never seen Brenna look more beautiful. From the moment she'd stepped off the elevator, he'd wanted to be alone with her, to slide that dark green dress from her delightful body and make love to her until they both needed resuscitation. And if the looks she'd given him throughout the evening were any indication, she was entertaining similar thoughts about him.

Wishing he could bypass the toast in favor of taking Brenna to his room, he lied, ''There's nothing that I'd like more than toasting your happiness.''

When they entered Pete and Abigail's suite a few minutes later, an ice bucket of champagne sat chilling beside a table in front of the sliding patio doors leading out to the balcony. Two long-stemmed wineglasses and a bowl of chocolate-coated strawberries sat waiting for the newly wedded couple's celebration.

''You do the honors while I get a couple more glasses,'' Pete said, handing Dylan the chilled bottle.

Popping the cork, he poured wine into the two crystal champagne flutes, then into the water glasses Pete had retrieved from the wet bar. Taking one of the water glasses, Dylan proposed a toast to the happiness and longevity of Pete and Abigail's marriage. The melodic ring of glass touching glass sealed the good wishes a moment before they all took a sip of the expensive champagne.

"Now, before we run you kids off to pursue your own good time, we have a confession to make," Abigail said, looking smug.

"Yep, and a request, too," Pete added as he reached for Abigail's hand.

Brenna took another sip of champagne, then looked at Dylan. He knew she wondered what the pair were driving at; the same as he was.

"What is it you have to confess?" he asked, not sure he wanted to know.

He watched Pete and Abigail exchange a look, a moment before Abigail cleared her throat. "You two didn't meet by accident. We set you up."

"You set us up?" Brenna asked, placing her glass on the table.

"Pete and I met a couple of days after you and I moved to Tranquillity," Abigail said, nodding. "Once we started talking about our families, it didn't take us any time at all to know that the two of you would be perfect for each other." She laughed. "And we've been arranging for you to spend time together ever since. We even took Dylan's truck, instead of your car for this trip because Pete said Dylan would come after it, and I knew you'd come with him."

"I've gone to the movie theater down in Alpine more in the last few weeks than I have in my whole life." Looking at Abigail, Pete grinned. "But spendin' all that time in the dark with Abby caused our matchmakin' to backfire."

"It serves the two of you right for trying to meddle,'' Brenna said good-naturedly. ''You can keep my car for your honeymoon and I'll ride back with Dylan.'' She turned to face him. ''If that's all right with you?''

Dylan nodded as he watched her reach for a chocolate-covered strawberry. When she popped the morsel into her mouth, then licked the juice from her fingers, it took everything he had in him not to groan out loud.

''What was the request?'' he asked, remembering the second reason the senior couple had wanted to talk to them. He braced himself. No telling what the pair had up their sleeves this time.

''With Christmas only a couple of weeks away, we ain't gonna have time to find a place of our own until after the holidays,'' Pete said, kissing the back of Abigail's wrinkled hand. ''We want you two to decide which one of you Abby and I are gonna live with until we move.''

''We don't want you to decide right now,'' Abigail quickly added. ''Talk it over on your way back to Tranquillity, then when Pete and I return from our honeymoon you can let us know.''

Dylan glanced at Brenna, then back at the newlyweds. ''I think it's safe to say you're welcome to stay with either one of us.''

''For as long as you want,'' Brenna added, reaching for another chocolate-covered strawberry. When she bit into it, Dylan had to glance away. The more he watched her lick her fingers, the tighter his body became.

''When we get back to town next week you can let us know what you've decided,'' Abigail said. She smiled at Pete. "As long as we're together, we don't care where we stay."

"Well, thanks for comin' to the weddin'," Pete said suddenly. "But it's time for you kids to skedaddle." He put his arm around Abigail. "Me and Abby ain't gettin' no younger and we got us a honeymoon to get started."

Brenna's cheeks turned beet-red and Dylan watched her down another strawberry before hugging her grandmother and his uncle Pete. "Congratulations. I'm very happy for both of you."

Dylan added his good wishes to Brenna's, then taking her by the hand, led her out into the hall and down the corridor. "Let's go see what's playing on the movie channels."

He glanced down at her as they waited for the elevator. With her alabaster complexion and copper-colored hair, Brenna looked utterly stunning in that dark green dress. But as good as she looked in it, Dylan knew beyond a shadow of doubt that she'd look better out of it.

When they stepped into the empty elevator and the doors closed, he pulled her into his arms. "I've wanted to kiss you ever since I saw you in the lobby," he said, brushing his lips over hers. "Do you know how beautiful you look tonight? How difficult it's been to keep my hands to myself?"

The smile she gave him damned near knocked his boots off. "Probably as difficult as it's been for me to keep my hands off you. Do you have any idea how yummy you look in black jeans and a sports coat?"

"Yummy?" He chuckled. "As yummy as chocolate-covered strawberries?"

She nodded. "Do you know why I kept eating those strawberries?"

"No."

The smile she gave him lit the darkest corners of his soul. "It was the next best thing to having you."

His blood surged through his veins and a spark ignited in his gut. "Darlin', if you keep saying things like that, I won't be held responsible for us missing whatever the movie channel is showing."

Grinning, she wrapped her arms around his waist and pressed herself against him. "Did I say I wanted to watch a movie? I'd rather watch you."

He felt his heart stop, then thump hard against his rib cage. "You're going to cause me to have a heart attack if you don't stop that."

"Stop what?" she asked innocently as they stepped off the elevator and started toward their room.

"You know what," he growled, digging in his jacket pocket for the card key.

"You don't want me to tell you how sexy I think you are?" she whispered close to his ear. "The other night at your place you said you wanted to hear me—"

"Not until we're in the room," he interrupted, fumbling with the key.

"Can I tell you how good it feels to have you—"

He placed his hand over her mouth, effectively cutting her off. "I've created a monster," he muttered, inserting the key into the slot.

She tickled his palm with her tongue and he damned near broke the card off in the lock. Pulling his hand from her mouth, he rubbed it against his thigh to ease the tingling sensation that sent his blood pressure skyrocketing and heat racing straight to the region below his belt buckle.

"Darlin', if you don't stop that I'm going to die of frustration before I get this door open."

"I was just going to tell you how good it feels to have you…"

He gave her a stern look.

She ignored it. "…here with me for Granny and Pete's wedding," she finished, her eyes twinkling mischievously.

"Oh, you're going to pay for that one," he promised as he finally opened the door to their room and turned on the lights. Pulling her inside, he took her into his arms as he kicked the door closed behind them. "Do you have any idea what that kind of talk can do to a man?"

"No." Her smile almost brought him to his knees. "Would you like to show me?"

At the sudden tightening of his groin, he sucked in a sharp breath. "You're determined to drive me out of my mind, aren't you?"

"I hadn't considered it," she said thoughtfully.

A spark of mischief lit her pretty blue eyes a moment before she walked over to the dimmer switch on the wall beside the door. Dimming the lights to a soft muted glow, she turned back to face him.

"But you drove me out of my mind last night in the hotel in Albuquerque, and the night before in your cabin, so I think it's only fair." Reaching up, she slipped the sports jacket from his shoulders and hung it in the closet. "Would you mind if I drove you a little crazy tonight, Sheriff?"

Dylan swallowed hard. "Not at all, darlin'."

She gave him a smile that caused his heart to stop, then take off at an alarming rate. "Tonight it's my turn to drive you to the brink."

His pulse thundered in his ears at the sparkling promise he saw in her determined gaze. Sensing that she needed to feel in control of their lovemaking, he forced himself to stand still while she worked at unbuttoning his shirt. Slowly easing the button below his open collar through the buttonhole, she trailed her fingers down his chest to the next button, then the next. He sucked in a sharp breath with each touch, and by the time she reached his waistband to tug the tails of his shirt from his jeans, he felt as if his lungs might explode.

Parting the fabric, she placed her hands on his stomach and lightly smoothed them up his abdomen to his chest. She teased his puckered nipples with her fingertips, then caressed his pectoral muscles with her soft, warm palms. Dylan exhaled the air trapped in his lungs in one big whoosh.

"Does that feel good?" she asked, glancing up at him from beneath her lashes.

He had to clear his throat to make his voice work. "If it felt any better I doubt I could stand it, darlin'."

She ran her hands up to his shoulders, then down his arms, pushing his shirt off as she went. "You have a beautiful body, Dylan."

Her softly murmured appreciation sent his temperature up several degrees. "I like yours a lot better," he said hoarsely.

The look she gave him when she tossed his shirt aside was filled with promise and he wondered what she'd do next. He didn't have long to wait. Taking him by the hand, she led him farther into the room, then walked over to turn on the clock-radio beside the bed. A slow romantic tune immediately surrounded them.

When she returned to stand in front of him, she bent to pull off his boots, then straightened to give him a look that made sweat bead on his forehead and his arousal strain against his fly. If the glint in her eyes was any indication, she fully intended to drive him stark raving mad with her exploration of his body before she once again allowed him a glimpse of her tempting curves.

Holding his gaze with hers, she ran her index finger down the narrow line of hair from his navel to his belt. Every muscle in his body tensed and he took a deep steadying breath. Standing still while Brenna had her fun just might prove to be the hardest thing he'd ever done. Her hands brushing his belly as she worked the leather strap through the metal buckle, had him placing his hands on her shoulders to steady himself. There was no question about it. It was *definitely* the most difficult thing he'd ever done.

He took several deep breaths in an effort to slow his body down. He'd be lucky if he had an ounce of sense left by the time she was finished undressing him, he decided.

She popped the snap on his jeans and toyed with the metal tab, causing him to swallow hard around the lump of cotton clogging his throat. He was aroused to an almost painful state and a zipper could be a lethal weapon to a man in his condition if it wasn't lowered carefully.

''Darlin'—''

Before he could warn her, she placed her finger to his lips, then slowly eased the tab down over the insistent bulge stretching his cotton briefs. He let out the breath he hadn't realized he'd been holding.

But when she touched the fabric covering his arousal, Dylan groaned and closed his eyes as the burning in his lower belly spread to every cell of his being. She was definitely driving him out of his mind. And heaven help him, he was loving every minute of it.

"Open your eyes and look at me, darling."

When he did as she commanded, she held his gaze with hers, placed her hands at his flanks, then slowly pushed his jeans and briefs from his hips and down his legs. Stepping out of them, he kicked them to the side and reached for her.

"Not yet." Her throaty whisper sent a wave of heat down his spine and he cursed himself for agreeing to let her play the role of seductress. He'd be lucky if he had a mind left at all by the time she finished with him.

She removed her shoes and panty hose, then arranging her long hair over one shoulder, turned for him to unzip the back of her dress. Aroused as he was, the simple task proved extremely difficult and he fumbled with the tab a moment before he finally managed to slide it open. His knuckles brushed her satiny smooth back and she trembled in response to his touch. She was as turned on as he was, and he took comfort in the fact that he wasn't the only one suffering from her loveplay.

Placing his hands on her shoulders, he turned her

to face him and started to take her into his arms. But she shook her head and stepped away from him.

He watched, mesmerized, as she slipped the dress from her creamy shoulders and let it fall into a dark green pool at her feet. Dylan swallowed hard when she reached up to release the front closure of her bra. The damned thing was so filmy he could see the deep rose of her tightly beaded nipples beneath the emerald-green lace.

She smiled as she unfastened the clasp, then slipped the straps down her arms, freeing her full, firm breasts to his appreciative gaze. He groaned. But when she hooked her thumbs in the waistband of her tiny panties, he thought his eyes would pop right out of his head. Besides her panty hose, all she'd had on beneath that pretty green dress the entire evening had been nothing but a wisp of lace that revealed more of her breasts than it covered, and a minuscule silk and lace thong. The knowledge caused the blood to roar through his veins and his body to jerk to full alert.

"I'm glad I didn't know about what you *didn't* have on under that dress, darlin'," he said, his voice sounding as if it had turned to rust.

Laughing softly, she walked toward him. "Why?"

"Because it would have been hard as hell to hide how much I want you," he growled. He held out his arms. "Come here, Brenna."

When she walked into his embrace, he pulled her to him and the feel of female against male, firm masculine flesh to soft feminine skin, had him feeling as if he'd been set on fire. He felt scored where her pebbled nipples pressed into his chest and his hard arousal nestled to her lower belly sent a rush of desire coursing through him that he thought might just take his head right off his shoulders.

"Dance with me," she whispered against his shoulder.

Dance? He was lucky he was still able to stand upright. But he'd walk through hellfire before he disappointed her, and when she began to gently sway against him, Dylan held her tight, gritted his teeth and fought to keep his sanity as he helped her play out her fantasy.

Tucking her long, silky hair behind her ear, he lowered his head and nibbled the sensitive skin along the column of her neck. Her moan of pleasure encouraged him and he slid his hands down her back to her bottom, then back up her sides to the swell of her breasts.

"Darlin', I want you more than I want my next breath."

She leaned back to look up at him, and the hunger he saw in her eyes sent a shaft of need straight to his groin. Taking his hand in hers, she led him to the bed. "Lie down, darling."

"Just a minute," he said, reaching for his discarded jeans. Removing a couple of the foil packets tucked in the back of his wallet, he placed them within easy reach on the beside table, then stretched out on the bed.

He expected her to join him, but instead she picked up one of the packets and tore it open. She hesitated, and he could tell she wasn't quite sure she had the nerve to finish the task.

"You're doin' just fine, darlin'," he said encouragingly.

His heart stuttered, then took off at a dead run when

her gaze met his a moment before she touched his fevered flesh and rolled their protection into place. He'd never had a woman do that and he found it more exciting than he'd ever dreamed possible.

He reached for her, but she shook her head. "Remember, it's my turn to drive you wild tonight, darling."

To his immense relief, not to mention the preservation of what was left of his mental health, she straddled him and without hesitation guided him to her moist heat. Closing his eyes, Dylan brought his hands up to hold her hips as her supple body consumed all of his. But Brenna's moan of pleasure as she completely settled herself on top of him almost proved his undoing and it took everything he had to keep what small scrap of control he had left.

"Darlin'…" He clenched his back teeth so tightly his jaw ached. "I'm not sure how much more of this I can handle."

"Open your eyes, Dylan," she said softly, repeating what he'd said to her the first night they'd made love.

When his gaze locked with hers, she began a gentle rocking that quickly had him racing toward the point of no return. Unable to contain himself any longer, he took control of the rhythm she'd set. Their bodies seemed to move in time with the music from the radio as he guided them to the pinnacle and he lost sight of where he ended and she began.

Seconds later, he felt her tighten around him, heard her brokenly whisper his name, a moment before she gave herself up to the culmination of pleasure. She collapsed on top of him and he held her trembling

body until the storm was spent and she went limp
with completion.

Only then did Dylan allow himself to succumb to
the red haze of passion surrounding him. Every muscle in his body constricted as he sought his own ful-
fillment, and surging into her a final time, he groaned
with the satisfaction of finding his own release from
the tension holding him captive.

Time seemed to stand still as Dylan slowly recov-
ered from the most soul-shattering climax of his life.
He'd never experienced anything like what he'd just
shared with Brenna.

"Dylan?"

"What, darlin'?"

"I love you," she said softly.

His heart skittered to a halt, then thumped hard
against his ribs as he came to terms with Brenna's
sleepy confession. Before he could form a response,
her even breathing signaled that she'd fallen asleep.

Had he heard her right? She loved him?

Dylan gently moved her to his side, then turned to
face her. Brushing a silky strand of copper hair from
her porcelain cheek, he watched her sleep. His chest
tightened and the spark of renewed desire began to
burn at his gut.

Brenna loved him.

Three weeks ago, that thought would have scared
him to death and sent him running in the opposite
direction. But now?

She snuggled against him in her sleep and Dylan
wrapped his arms around her to cradle her to him. A
protectiveness he'd never felt before swept
through him.

He took a deep breath, then another.

Five years ago, he'd made a fool of himself, and the fear of doing it again had kept him from getting involved with anyone since. But Brenna wasn't just any other woman. She was fast becoming an obsession, a necessity in his life that he hadn't known existed.

He gazed down at her. Somehow she'd gotten under his skin without him realizing when or how. And if the tender, protective feelings he had welling up inside of him were any indication, she'd be there for a good long time.

Nine

Four days after she and Dylan returned from Las Vegas, Brenna sat in the community room of the town hall, staring off into space. Her mind wasn't on the Beautification Society's committee meeting, the second phase of the project, or the complaints the women mentioned getting from their husbands about the Santa Claus fire hydrants. All she'd been able to think about for the past few days had been Dylan and where their relationship was headed.

After they'd made love the night they'd spent in Las Vegas, she'd inadvertently told him she loved him before she'd fallen asleep. She hadn't meant to let him know how she felt, but once the words were out, there was no turning back.

He'd remained silent, and neither one of them had mentioned it, even though they'd spent every spare minute of the day together, and every night entwined in each other's arms since being trapped in his cabin the day the blue norther blew through. And that bothered her. A lot.

When she'd been involved with Tom, he'd been the first to tell her how he felt. But Tom had turned out to be self-centered, and she'd learned the hard way that his feelings for her were as shallow as he was.

But Dylan was different. He didn't have an agenda, a scheme to further his plans at her expense. His career was secure and there wasn't anything he needed from her. She sighed. Unfortunately, that still didn't alter the fact that he knew how she felt about him, while she had no idea what his feelings were for her.

"Brenna, dear, are you listening?" Cornelia asked, interrupting Brenna's disturbing introspection.

"I'm sorry." Brenna sat up straight and faced the other ladies of the planning committee sitting across the table from her. "What was that you were saying? Some of the men are complaining about the fire hydrants?"

Emily Taylor nodded. "When I told my Ed that we intend to paint them for every holiday, I thought he was going to choke on his supper." The woman shook her head. "I can't understand what the men are so upset about. They're just fire hydrants."

"Have any of you told your husbands what we plan to do for the week preceding the Christmas Jamboree?" Brenna asked, feeling a tension headache coming on. She certainly didn't want to continue the project if the men were all opposed to more changes.

"No," Helen Washburn said, looking grim. "Luke

and I haven't been on real good terms since he told me to throw away my paints and buy a dog to occupy my time." She snorted. "He tried to get back in my good graces with a box of chocolates a couple of days later, but he never did apologize."

"Ed did the same thing," Emily said, frowning.

Cornelia's eyes narrowed. "Myron did, too."

Brenna rubbed the throbbing at her temples. "If it's going to be this much of a problem, maybe we should scrap the rest of the project."

"We'll do no such thing," Cornelia stated flatly. She rose from her seat to pace back and forth a moment before she stopped to plant her fists on her ample hips. "The men in this town have had their way and run things long enough. And it's time we put a stop to it."

"We're citizens of Tranquillity the same as they are," Emily said, nodding.

"That's right," Helen agreed. "My family's been here a lot longer than Luke's."

Brenna listened to the exchange with a growing sense of trepidation. It sounded like the women were planning to take over the town, instead of decorate Main Street for the community Christmas party.

"Girls, we're going to proceed as planned, and the devil take what the men think," Cornelia said, slapping the tabletop with the flat of her hand.

"Ladies, I'm not sure that's such a good idea," Brenna said, hoping to defuse the mutiny. "If the men don't want the Beautification Society painting new street signs and renaming Main Street 'Reindeer Way' for the next week—"

"Don't worry about the men," Cornelia interrupted, laughing. "They're not going to know anything about it until it's a done deal. Tomorrow's Saturday and we'll have all day to work on them. We'll meet here first thing in the morning, lock the doors and paint the signs, then we'll divide into teams and put them up simultaneously. By the time the men notice what we're doing, we'll be finished."

"I'm all for it," Helen said, looking quite pleased.

"Me, too." Emily clapped her hands excitedly. "Cornelia, you're a genius."

If the men were protesting the painting of a handful of fire hydrants, what would happen when the women painted wooden cut-outs of reindeer and tacked them over the existing street signs all along Tranquillity's main thoroughfare?

"But don't we have to have permission from the town council to implement a change like that?" Brenna asked, hoping that reason would prevail.

"Not as far as I'm concerned," Cornelia said confidently. She grinned wickedly as she added, "If Myron says anything about our putting the signs up, I've got a couch that he considers an instrument of torture. If he has to spend a night or two on it, he'll shut up soon enough."

"What's wrong, darlin'?" Dylan asked as he helped Brenna hang ornaments on the Christmas tree he'd helped her set up in front of her living room window. She'd been strangely quiet all evening and he could tell something was bothering her. Bad.

She sighed heavily and the sound caused his chest to tighten. He didn't like the idea of anything upsetting her.

"I met with the Beautification Society's planning committee this afternoon."

At the mention of the B.S. Club, Dylan's eyebrow started to twitch and his gut twisted into a tight knot. How the hell was he going to get out of hearing about the Main Street Project this time?

If he'd known Brenna was troubled by something the B.S. Club had up their sleeves, he'd have kept his mouth shut. The less he knew about their cockamamie schemes, the better. That way, the next time Myron asked if Brenna had divulged any information about the second phase of the project, Dylan could honestly say that she hadn't.

"Do you know why some of the men are so upset by the Main Street Project?" she asked as she hung ornaments that looked like little miniature lassoes on the branches.

The twitch in his eyebrow increased. "What makes you think they're upset?" he asked, positioning a gold star on the top of the tree.

She turned to face him and her worried expression tightened the knot in his stomach. "The members of the committee said their husbands thought the idea of painting the fire hydrants for different holidays was ludicrous."

He swallowed hard. What could he say? He thought the damned things were pretty ridiculous, too.

"Most of the men in Tranquillity have been here all their lives," he said, choosing his words carefully. "They like the way the town has always been and don't see any reason to change it."

He watched her digest what he'd said, then shake her head. "The women don't want to change Tranquillity's way of life. They just want to liven it up a bit by putting up a few seasonal decorations to make its celebrations more special.''

"Like the Jamboree?"

Hanging a tiny Christmas stocking on one of the branches, she nodded. "Painting fire hydrants and—''

Before she could finish telling him something he'd rather not know, Dylan reached out and pulled her into his arms. "Don't worry about it, darlin'. Everyone will have a good time at the Jamboree just like they always do.''

"But—''

He covered her mouth with his, effectively putting an end to any further talk of fire hydrants, the B.S. Club, or anything else. By the time he lifted his head, the worried expression on Brenna's face had disappeared.

Stepping away from her, he took a deep breath to slow his body's response to the kiss. The sooner they finished decorating the tree, the sooner he could do what he really wanted. And that was to carry her to the bedroom and make love to her for the rest of the night.

"Have you heard from the newlyweds?" he asked, picking up a strand of garland that looked like a string of red peppers. He grinned. Apparently, Brenna wanted her tree's theme to reflect her recent move to southwest Texas.

Nodding, she pulled a sprig of fake mistletoe from a sack. "Granny called this afternoon to say they'd be spending tomorrow night in Albuquerque, then drive home the day after.''

"Have you thought about which one of us they'll stay with until they find a place?" he asked, draping the garland over the branches.

"Not really," she said as she looked around for a place to hang the mistletoe. "I wish they hadn't put the burden of making a choice on us."

"I guess we could take turns." He shrugged. "One week here. One week out at my place."

"That would work," Brenna said, sounding distracted.

Dylan glanced up to see her worrying her lower lip. "What's wrong?"

"I can't seem to find a place to hang the mistletoe," she said, frowning.

"Let me see what I can come up with." He took the sprig of greenery from her and held it over her head. Grinning, he leaned down to kiss her soft, sweet lips. "I like hanging it right here."

On Sunday afternoon, Dylan sat in his private office, staring at the three grim-faced men on the other side of his desk. "Myron, did you give the B.S. Club permission for this latest change?" he asked tiredly.

"Hell no!" Apparently unable to sit still, the mayor shot from his chair to pace the perimeter of the room. "The first I heard about it was when Luke called to tell me to look out my window at the street sign on the corner."

"Whoever heard of a town in southwest Texas with the main road runnin' through it named Reindeer Way?" Luke asked, sounding as disgusted as he looked. "Hell, unless they got one in the zoo in El

Paso, or up in Dallas, there ain't a reindeer within two thousand miles of here.''

Ed snorted. ''And the women have it in their heads they're gonna do somethin' like this for every holiday.'' His face reddened and the veins on the side of his neck stood out as his anger rose. ''Emily said they're already makin' plans to paint the hydrants to look like rabbits for Easter, leprechauns for St. Patrick's Day and cupids for Valentine's Day.''

''No tellin' what else they'll come up with,'' Luke said, groaning.

Clearly exasperated, Myron took off his cowboy hat and ran an agitated hand over his bald head. ''Knowin' Cornelia and that bunch, they'll end up callin' Main Street somethin' stupid like the Bunny Trail or Leprechaun Lane.''

Ed's face turned a deeper shade of crimson. ''Aw, hell. You don't think they'll try to put some kind of canopy over Main Street and call it the Tunnel of Love for Valentine's Day, do you?''

Dylan reached up to rub his twitching eyebrow as he listened to the men bluster about the street signs along Main Street. He'd thought the Santa fire hydrants were tacky, but they couldn't hold a candle to the painted, wooden reindeer street signs the B.S. Club had put up. The damned things had the sappiest grins plastered on their faces that he'd ever seen. He could only imagine what the women would do with bunnies, leprechauns and cupids.

''If you didn't give them permission to do this, Myron, then who did?'' Dylan asked tiredly.

''That's the real kicker in all this,'' Ed said, looking bewildered. ''They just up and did it without checkin' with any of us.'' He shook his head. ''They've never done that before.''

''You know, Dylan, most of this is your fault,'' Myron said, sinking back down in his chair.

''My fault! How do you figure that?'' Dylan demanded, his gut feeling as if he'd been sucker punched.

Ed nodded. ''We told you to spend as much time as you could with that Montgomery gal and find out what the B.S. Club was up to.''

''Yeah,'' Luke chimed in. ''You were supposed to let us know what the women had up their sleeves so we could stop it before it went this far.''

''Take that little gal down to a movie in Alpine this evenin','' Myron said. ''And while you're sittin' in the dark all cuddled up, find out if they're plannin' anything else.''

''Yeah,'' Ed said, crossing his arms over his chest. ''If my face ends up on a leprechaun or a cupid, your job just might depend on it.''

Before he could defend himself, Dylan heard a quiet gasp. Looking up, his heart felt as if it dropped to his boottops. There stood Brenna at the open door of his office, her face ashen.

''I'm sorry…the door was open and I—'' She stopped to take a breath. ''I have to go now.''

Her eyes met his then, and the shattered expression on her beautiful face tore at his insides. Jumping to his feet, he started around the desk. ''Brenna—''

But she'd already whirled around and fled.

Brenna ran across the outer room of the sheriff's office, shoved through the door, then started down the sidewalk. Her heart pounded and her chest felt too constricted to breathe. Dylan had only been seeing her because he'd been ordered to discover what he could about the Main Street Project and report back to the town council.

Tears blurred her vision, but she kept on running. He'd followed the directive and spent as much time as he could with her in his effort to carry out his mission. And like a fool, she'd played right into his hand.

Pain as sharp as if a knife had been plunged into her chest made her stop to wrap her arms around herself. No wonder he hadn't told her he loved her. He didn't. Dylan had only been seeing her to ensure his position as sheriff was secure. Her breath caught on a sob. He'd used her, just as Tom had done.

Feeling as if she might be physically ill, Brenna started down the side street leading to her house. But she'd only gone a few yards when two strong hands clamped down on her shoulders to stop her.

"Darlin'—"

"Don't call me that," she said around the lump clogging her throat. Whirling to face Dylan, she gritted her teeth as she fought the emotions churning inside of her. "Don't ever call me that again."

"I need to explain about—"

"You don't have to justify yourself, *Sheriff*. You were just following orders." Squirming from beneath his tight grasp, she once again started toward home.

"Dammit, Brenna, be reasonable," he said, falling into step beside her.

"Go away."

"No. Not until you listen."

"There's nothing you can say that will make a difference," she said, fighting with everything she had not to cry.

When she reached her yard, she hurried toward the sanctuary of her home. Once she went inside and bolted the door, she could let her pent-up emotions break free without Dylan seeing how badly he'd hurt her.

But he stopped her by placing his hand flat on the door to hold it shut when she tried to open it. She struggled to pull it free, but no amount of tugging on her part would budge him.

"Dammit, Brenna, you're going to hear me out," he said, his expression a mixture of anger and frustration.

Turning on him, she shook her head. "No, I'm not."

"Yes, you are," he said, taking hold of her upper arms.

To her frustration, tears began to fill her eyes. She blinked them away. She would not let him see her cry. "What's the point, Dylan? Are you hoping to assuage your conscience? Do you think that will make you feel better about what you've done?"

"I haven't done anything," he insisted.

Emotional pain like she'd never known tore through her. "Oh, really? You didn't follow orders? You haven't been with me for the past four weeks, hoping to learn something the men could use to stop the Main Street Project?"

"It wasn't like that," he said, shaking his head. "Yes, I was told to find out what you knew about the women's plans. But if you'll remember, I never questioned you about it.''

''Because you didn't ask me about it, you think that makes what you've done all right?'' she asked incredulously. ''You kissed me, you made love to me only because you were ordered to spend time with me.'' Her voice shook, but she didn't care. ''Do you have any idea how that makes me feel? How much it hurts to know that I gave myself to a man who was only using me in order to keep his job?''

''Now hold it right there, Brenna,'' he said, looking angry. ''What we have between us is real and has nothing to do with the orders I was given, the B.S. Club or the town. I've been with you because I wanted to be, because I care for you.''

''I wish I could believe that, Dylan,'' she said, feeling as if her heart was being torn in two. ''But I don't.''

''It's the truth,'' he said stubbornly. ''And if you'll think back, every time you started to talk about the project, I changed the subject.''

She shook her head. ''It doesn't matter. The fact remains that you allowed those men to think your role in all this was the reason for our being together. Not because you cared for me. You used me the same as Tom did.''

''No, I didn't,'' Dylan insisted. ''What goes on between the two of us is none of the council's business.'' He took a deep breath. ''Five years ago, I started seeing a woman who used my attraction to her in an effort to turn Tranquillity into a resort for people who have more money than good sense. She made a fool of me in front of the entire town. And believe me, I'd never put you through that kind of hell."

"But you just did," Brenna said, pulling from his grasp. She shuddered from the strain of holding back the torrent of emotions threatening to break through. "I'm sorry I stumbled onto the scheme before you had the chance to make sure that your job was secure. Maybe the council members will take that into consideration when it's time for your next evaluation."

"Darlin'—"

"Please don't," she interrupted, opening the door. "There's nothing left to say." Brenna took a deep breath in an effort to hold back her tears. "Granny and Pete should get home from their honeymoon sometime this evening. When they arrive, I'll have Pete give you a call."

"This isn't over, Brenna."

"Yes, it is." She had to get away from him before she fell completely apart. "Goodbye, Dylan."

Her heart breaking into a million pieces, Brenna entered the house, closed the door behind her, then leaned back against it. Shaking uncontrollably, she sank to the living room floor and covered her face with her hands. But when she heard the sound of Dylan's footsteps as he walked down the steps, as he walked away from her, the last of her control snapped and she gave free rein to the flood of tears she could no longer hold in check.

Dylan slowly descended the steps and started walking the six blocks back to the center of town. Was he guilty of what Brenna had accused him of? In his effort to maintain their privacy, had he cheapened the relationship they'd developed between them with his silence? Had he betrayed her trust by not making it clear to Myron and the council members that he had been seeing her because he wanted to, not because he'd been ordered to?

Since that incident five years ago, he'd done his damnedest to keep his private life separate from his position as sheriff. And up until the last month, he'd been successful.

But that was before everyone he knew started meddling in his and Brenna's lives. At first it had been his uncle and her grandmother playing matchmakers in order to get them together. Then when the mayor's wife and a handful of her friends decided to make a few harmless changes around town, the town council had gotten in on the act and ordered him to find out what Brenna knew in their effort to stop their wives.

And despite all the interference, all the subterfuge, he and Brenna had managed to fall in love.

Dylan stopped dead in his tracks. He took a deep breath, then another. He knew she'd gotten under his skin. But when had he fallen in love with her?

He shook his head as he resumed walking. It didn't matter when he'd given Brenna his heart. He had. And he'd be damned before he let any more well-meaning souls destroy what they had between them.

He smiled determinedly. And that included Brenna.

Ten

On Christmas Eve, Brenna sat staring at the huge bowl of chocolate rum balls her grandmother placed on the table in front of her. For the first time in her life, Brenna wasn't even tempted by the taste of chocolate.

"Pete, cover that bowl with plastic wrap while I cut the fudge," Abigail instructed. Stopping to adjust her Santa hat, she turned to Brenna. "You'd better start getting ready for the Jubilee."

"Jamboree," Brenna corrected.

"Whatever," her grandmother said, waving her hand dismissively. "If you don't get the lead out you're going to be late."

Brenna shook her head as she rose to go to her room. "I'm not going."

"You have to go, Brenna," Pete said, struggling

to tear the plastic wrap from the carton. "If you don't, who's gonna read to the kids?"

"Anyone can read *'Twas the Night Before Christmas* and the children will listen," she said shrugging.

"But you're the Story Lady," Pete argued. Brenna watched him exchange a look with her grandmother, then place the box of plastic wrap on the table. "I think I'll mosey on into the livin' room to…to…" He paused for a moment, then grinned sheepishly. "Aw, shoot. I'll find somethin' to do."

Brenna watched him kiss Abigail's cheek, then saunter from the room. "You can save your breath, Granny," she said, anticipating Abigail's argument that she attend the community party. "I'm not going."

Abigail motioned for her to sit down at the table, then plopped down in the chair across from her. "Brenna, as long as you continue living in Tranquillity you're going to run into Dylan from time to time." Leave it to her grandmother to cut right to the heart of the matter.

"It's just…" Brenna took a deep breath. "It's too soon."

"I know it hurts, honey," Abigail said, reaching out to cover Brenna's hand with hers. "But you have to face seeing him sometime. And the longer you put it off, the harder it's going to be when you do."

Moisture filled her eyes, but Brenna blinked it away. She'd already cried enough in the past week to fill a river, and she was determined not to shed another tear. "Maybe I'll move."

Abigail snorted and said a word that under different

circumstances would have shocked Brenna. "I didn't raise you to run from your problems."

"I'm not running from them," Brenna said defensively. "I'm just trying to survive them."

"Then face them head-on, deal with what you have to and move forward," Abigail said staunchly. "Show this town what kind of backbone you have."

Brenna shrugged. "That's what Cornelia said when she stopped by the shop this morning to tell me how sorry she was for what her husband and the town council tried to do."

"How many times does that make?"

"Between Cornelia, Emily Taylor and Helen Washburn, I've been apologized to every day this week." Brenna shook her head. "How could something as harmless as painting a few fire hydrants and putting up a handful of decorative signs cause so many problems?"

"I don't know." Her grandmother shook her head. "When Pete dropped by Luke's yesterday afternoon, he said the men were all stopping in for their supper." At Brenna's questioning look, Abigail laughed. "Apparently Cornelia, Emily and Helen are getting even with their husbands by refusing to cook. And Myron Worthington is hobbling around, complaining to anyone who will listen to him about a loose spring in a sofa."

Brenna groaned. "This power struggle between the women and men just keeps getting worse."

Grinning, Abigail nodded. "I can't wait to see what happens tonight."

"Granny!"

"Nothing like a good feud to liven up a party,"

Abigail said, rising to her feet. "Now, go get ready or you'll miss the fun."

"I might as well," Brenna said, sighing heavily as she rose to her feet. "You're not going to let me alone until I do, are you?"

"Nope." Abigail shook her head so vigorously that her bright orange curls bounced beneath her Santa hat. "Besides, it would be a waste of a good elf costume if you don't go."

Brenna shook her head as she walked into her room. She should have known her grandmother would keep after her until she gave in and got ready for the party.

As she slipped into the short elf dress, tights and green high-heeled boots with white fur trim, one thing kept running through her mind. Dylan would be at the celebration.

She bit her lower lip to stop its trembling as she tied the big red bows at the top of her boots. In the past week, she'd thought a lot about what he'd told her after she stumbled across the meeting being held in his office.

It was true that he'd never questioned her about the Main Street Project. In fact, he had avoided any mention of it, unless she brought it up. And reliving every moment of their time together, she had to admit that he'd never allowed her to tell him what the women were planning. He'd either quickly changed the subject, or kissed her into silence every time she'd tried to talk about the project.

After thinking of nothing else for an entire week, she'd even come to terms with, and understood, the precarious position he'd found himself in with the town council. He'd been stuck in the middle of the whole mess and forced to walk a fine line in order to keep everyone happy. Not an easy place to be, nor was it an easy task to undertake.

On one hand, he'd been trying to placate the mayor and town council members in order to keep a job he loved. And on the other hand, he'd tried his best not to betray her faith and trust in him while sidestepping their directive.

And she'd even come to understand his not making the councilmen aware of his relationship with her. After suffering the public humiliation he'd been forced to endure five years ago, she couldn't blame him for wanting to keep that part of his life private.

But all of her realization had come too late. She hadn't seen or heard from Dylan in a week. If that didn't speak volumes about his reluctance to give their relationship another chance, she didn't know what did.

Her breath caught on a soft sob. There was no way she could spend the entire evening watching Dylan, loving him, and not humiliate herself by falling apart.

She felt a tear trickle down her cheek and impatiently wiped it away with the back of her hand. She'd appease everyone and attend the Christmas Jamboree tonight, but she wouldn't stay. She'd read a story to the children, help whoever played Santa pass out the presents, then leave.

Dylan stood on the far side of the community room, watching the door, and the minute Brenna, Pete and Abigail walked in, his body tensed. He damned near crushed his cup of punch. Brenna looked good in the little green elf dress with white fur trim. Damned good. But as far as he was concerned, she looked good in, or out of, just about anything she wore.

The skirt brushed the middle of her thighs and the fluffy white fur around the collar touched her satiny smooth skin like he longed to do. His body tightened. He'd like nothing more than to throw her over his shoulder, find a nice secluded spot and make love to her until she came to her senses.

He barely managed to swallow back the groan threatening to escape. He'd decided to give her some time before he tried to once again get through to her. But how was he ever going to get through the evening without holding her, loving her?

"How's it goin', boy?" Pete asked, strolling over to stand next to him.

"About the same." Dylan took a swig of punch from the bent plastic cup. "How are things with you, Uncle Pete?"

"Good." They stood in silence for several minutes before his uncle shook his head. "Dang it, why don't you come right out and ask?"

Dylan feigned ignorance as he watched old Corny and her hens surround Brenna, then usher her over to where they'd been sitting. "Ask what?"

Pete snorted. "Aw, hell, boy. We both know you're dyin' to know about Brenna. Why don't you stop pussyfootin' around and ask me?"

Unable to take his eyes off her, Dylan shrugged. "Then why don't you just tell me and save both of us some time, Uncle Pete?"

"All righty, I will," Pete said, sounding irritated. "She's about the most miserable little gal I think I

ever did see. Abby had to talk herself blue, just to get
Brenna to come here tonight.''

Dylan's gut twisted. Knowing that he'd been the
cause of her misery just about tore him apart. ''She
wasn't going to attend the Jamboree?''

''Nope.'' Pete rocked back on his heels. ''And in
case anybody wants to know, it wouldn't surprise me
if she don't hightail it out of here as soon as she reads
to the kids and helps pass out presents.''

''Looks like the feud is still in full swing,'' Abigail
said, coming to stand next to Pete. ''With the women
on one side of the room and the men huddled up on
the other, I'd say the battlelines are drawn.''

Dylan had heard, first hand, about all the trouble
Myron, Ed and Luke had encountered when their
wives learned of their plot to end the Main Street
Project. All week long, he'd listened to Myron whine
about sleeping on that damned couch, until Dylan had
been ready to go out and buy the man another one
just to shut him up. And when Ed and Luke arrived
earlier in the evening with Emily and Helen, they'd
immediately split up with the women going one way
and the men another.

''Pete, let's grab those two chairs over by the
punch bowl,'' Abigail said excitedly. ''Unless I miss
my guess, something's about to pop loose and I want
a good seat.''

As Pete and Abigail hurried across the room to the
chairs lined against the wall closest to the refreshment
table, Dylan watched Brenna and the women walk
over to the punch bowl. Glancing in the opposite direction, he saw the men head straight for them. It
looked like Abigail was right, he decided when Cor-

nelia and her hens started bobbing their heads and pointing their fingers, while Myron, Ed and Luke wore deep scowls and shook their heads in obvious disagreement.

Dylan watched as Brenna stood in the middle of all of it, her head turning from one side to the other as the debate heated up. She looked helpless and on the verge of tears.

"That's it," he said, tossing the cup in the trash as he walked toward the gathering crowd and the woman he loved.

Brenna cringed as the knot of people gathering in front of the refreshment table grew. It seemed that everyone had an opinion about the fire hydrants and street signs.

"I like the changes," a woman spoke up from the edge of the crowd. "I can't wait to see what the Beautification Society does for other holidays."

"How in the name of Sam Hill can you say that?" a man's voice countered disgustedly. "They're the silliest things I've ever laid eyes on."

"Please don't argue," Brenna said, in an effort to stop the escalating debate. But her voice was lost in all the noise as everyone stated their feelings.

"It's all her fault," an angry male voice rose above the din. "If she hadn't got the B.S. Club all stirred up, this never woulda happened."

"Now, hold it right there!"

At the sound of Dylan's baritone booming over the bedlam, Brenna looked up to see him shouldering his way toward her.

When she'd first walked into the community room,

she'd seen him standing alone on the far side of the room. She'd noticed that he had on the blue sports jacket and black jeans that he'd worn for her grandmother and Pete's wedding. He'd looked so handsome that she'd had to look away.

After that, she'd carefully avoided looking his direction. It simply hurt too much to love him, knowing there was no chance for them to work things out between them.

When he walked up to her, the brim of his black Resistol dipped slightly as he gave her an almost imperceptible nod. Her heart skipped a beat. What was he going to do?

Turning to face the crowd, he shook his head. "Brenna Montgomery didn't start this fight by teaching the women how to paint, or by taking charge when they *asked* for her help." He glanced down at her and the intense determination in his green eyes stole her breath. He was coming to her defense. "The only thing she's guilty of is wanting to find her place in Tranquillity and trying to become one of us." He pushed the brim of his hat up with his thumb, then propped his fists on his hips as he frowned at the crowd. "Although judging by the way you're all acting this evening, it's a mystery to me why she'd even want to bother."

She watched in disbelief as he pulled the lapel of his sports jacket aside to remove the silver star pinned to his shirt. "Dylan?"

The smile he gave her brought tears to her eyes. "It's all right, darlin'." Turning to the mayor, Dylan tossed the man his badge. "I've been proud to serve Tranquillity for the past six years, but when the town becomes more important than the people in it, I'm done."

Obviously dumbstruck, everyone fell silent as they awaited a reaction from Myron Worthington. The only sound in the room came from a group of small children playing in the corner close to the Christmas tree.

"Now, Dylan—"

Dylan shook his head as he put his arm around Brenna's shoulders. "Myron, when it comes to a choice between this town and the woman I love, there's no contest. Tranquillity will come in a distant second every time."

Brenna felt as if the floor had dropped from beneath her feet and she wasn't sure she'd heard him correctly. Had Dylan just admitted he loved her in front of the entire town?

But she couldn't allow him to give up his job as sheriff. It meant too much to him.

Reaching out, she took the badge from the mayor and handed it back to Dylan. "I can't let you do this, Dylan." Her voice caught, but she pressed on as she turned back to face the crowd. "I know how much Dylan loves Tranquillity. How much he loves all of you. And being your sheriff means too much to him for me to let him resign."

"Darlin'—"

She placed her finger to his lips. "I'll take full responsibility for the fire hydrants and street signs, and I'll even close my shop and leave if that's what it takes to restore peace to the town." She rose up on tiptoes to brush his lips with hers. "But I can't let them accept your resignation. I love you too much for that, Dylan.''

''Oh, that's the sweetest thing I've ever heard,'' Cornelia said tearfully. Turning to her husband, she demanded, ''Myron, say something.''

''Now…now, see here,'' the man stammered. ''There's no reason for anybody to go quittin' their job or leavin' town.''

''No reason at all,'' Luke Washburn said, his eyes looking slightly moist.

''Put that badge back on, Dylan,'' Ed Taylor said, his voice hoarse. ''We'll work this out.''

Dylan pulled her into his arms. ''What do you say, Brenna? Are we going to be able to work all this out?''

Tears flowed down her cheeks as Brenna gazed up at the man she loved with all her heart. ''I think there's a good probability that we will,'' she said, smiling.

''Good enough for me,'' he said, his heated gaze sending a shiver of longing down her spine. ''Darlin', will you do me the honor of being my wife?''

If Brenna thought the room fell silent when Dylan handed the mayor his badge, it couldn't compare to the hush that fell over the crowd as they awaited her answer. Even the children milling around the Christmas tree in the corner seemed to pause as if they sensed something significant was about to take place.

Tears ran unchecked down her cheeks as she threw her arms around his neck. ''Dylan, if it were possible, I'd marry you right here, tonight. Yes, I'll be your wife.''

An immediate cheer rose from the citizens of Tranquillity and it took several minutes for everyone to settle down after congratulating the happy couple.

"Brenna?"

Turning at the sound of her name, Brenna watched Mildred Bruner come forward. "Did you mean it when you said you'd marry Dylan tonight if it were possible?"

Glancing up at his handsome face, Brenna turned back to Mildred. "Yes, I would."

"What about you, dear?" Mildred asked Dylan.

Brenna watched him nod without hesitation. "I wish we could get married tonight, Mildred. But as county clerk, you know there's a three-day waiting period from the time the marriage license is issued until a couple can exchange vows."

"That's true," the woman admitted. "But if a district judge waives the waiting period, a couple can get married right away."

His grin wide, Pete walked up to slap Dylan on the back at the same time Abigail hugged Brenna. "Judge Bertrand's ranch is only seven miles from here," Pete said thoughtfully.

"He owes me a favor," Myron said, looking pleased. "Me, Ed and Luke can take a run up that way and have him back here in an hour."

Dylan gave Brenna a look that curled her toes inside her green Christmas boots. "Do you still carry your book of certificates with you, Mildred?" he asked.

Mildred nodded. "A body never knows when it might come in handy."

His slow grin made Brenna's heart skip a beat.

"What do you say, darlin'? Would you like to get married tonight?"

"Yes," she said without a moment's hesitation.

Dylan gave her a quick kiss a moment before everyone seemed to start talking at once.

Cornelia stepped forward, and barking orders that would have made any wedding planner proud, took charge. Dispatching Myron, Ed and Luke to get the judge, she set the ladies of the Beautification Society to the task of turning the Christmas Jamboree into a wedding, while an ecstatic Abigail hustled Brenna home to change out of the elf costume.

An hour later, wearing the green dress she'd worn for Pete and her grandmother's wedding, and holding a bouquet of red and white silk rosebuds, Brenna stood in the hallway outside of the community room.

"Brenna, you make a mighty pretty bride," Pete said, his faded blue eyes suspiciously bright.

"Of course, she does, you old goat." Abigail placed a garland of white baby's breath on Brenna's head. "She's my granddaughter."

Pete chuckled. "And Dylan's a handsome young buck because he's my nephew."

"I can't believe this is happening," Brenna murmured, her head spinning from the events of the last hour.

The muted sound of "Here Comes the Bride" filtered from the community room a moment before Cornelia opened the door. "Your groom awaits, Brenna."

Abigail gave her a watery smile and patted her

cheek, then turned and slowly walked through the door.

"Ready, gal?" Pete asked, holding his arm out for her to take.

Tucking her hand in the crook of his arm, Brenna nodded. "I've never been more ready for anything in my life."

When Pete escorted her through the door, the citizens of Tranquillity parted into two groups to form an aisle. Brenna looked for, and found, Dylan standing next to Judge Bertrand on the far side of the candlelit room by the Christmas tree. Lights on the tree twinkled behind him, but she barely noticed. The glow of love she saw in his emerald eyes held her captive as she walked toward the man she loved.

"Are you ready to make this a Christmas Jamboree that Tranquillity will never forget?" Dylan asked as he took her hand from Pete.

"I've never been more ready for anything in my life," she said, tears of happiness blurring her vision. "I love you, Dylan Chandler."

"And I love you, darlin'." He placed a soft kiss on the back of her hand, then giving her a smile that warmed her all the way to her soul, he said, "Let's get married."

Epilogue

Christmas Eve, one year later

Dylan smiled fondly as he watched Brenna slowly lower herself into a chair beside the Christmas tree, then pick up the book she'd selected to read to the kids before Santa Claus made his big entrance at the Christmas Jamboree. He'd have never believed it possible, but he loved her more today than he had the day he'd made her his wife.

"Brenna looks very pretty tonight," Mayor Worthington said, coming to stand next to Dylan.

"Yes, she does, Cornelia," he said proudly. He glanced over at the first female elected to the position of mayor in Tranquillity's one hundred and fifty year history. "Where's Myron?"

"He's putting on his suit." Cornelia laughed. "He

complained that it's a tradition for the mayor to play Santa at the Jamboree, but the council members and I decided that it would be best if he continued, since I wouldn't be as convincing as he is.''

Dylan grinned. ''I heard the women also voted to have Luke and Ed play Santa's helpers this year, too.''

''Emily made the motion and Helen seconded it,'' Cornelia said, giving him a smug smile.

Cornelia moved on to talk to some of her other constituents and Dylan turned his attention back to watching Brenna. When she finally closed the over-size book she'd been reading, Santa Claus appeared at the back of the room, right on cue, and the kids turned their attention on Myron and his two disgruntled-looking elves as they carried brightly wrapped presents to place under the Christmas tree.

As Pete and Abigail passed him on their way to the punch bowl, Pete laughed. ''Did you ever see a more bowlegged elf than Ed Taylor?''

Laughing Dylan shook his head. ''In those green tights, he's a real sight, that's for sure.''

''If you ask me, Luke's the one who's a sight,'' Abigail said, pointing toward the three men passing out presents. ''There's a good two inches of his belly shining between the bottom of his green T-shirt and the top of his pants.''

''What time is it?'' Brenna asked, waddling over to join them.

Checking his watch, Dylan told her the time, then placed his arms around her shoulders. ''Are you getting tired?''

She shook her head as she placed her hand over her swollen belly. ''No. Just checking.''

"This is a lot different than last year's Jubilee, isn't it?" Abigail asked, sounding disappointed.

"Jamboree," Brenna, Dylan and Pete corrected in unison.

"Whatever." Abigail waved her hand dismissively. "It's not nearly as exciting. Nobody's feuding and no one's getting married."

"It can't be excitin' every year, sugar," Pete said, kissing Abigail's cheek.

Dylan hugged Brenna close, then kissed the top of her head. "As far as I'm concerned, there will never be another Jamboree as special as that one."

"Never say never," Brenna said, laughing breathlessly.

"So what did the doctor tell you today?" Abigail asked. "Is my first great-grandchild going to be a Christmas baby or a New Year's baby?"

Smiling down at the woman he loved more than life itself, Dylan covered Brenna's hand where it rested over their child. "He said it could be any time."

Brenna nodded. "All we know for sure is that the baby is a little girl."

"A girl?" Pete grinned. "If she's as pretty as her momma and great-grandma, we'll be beatin' the boys back with a stick, Dylan."

Dylan's eyebrow began to twitch and his gut twisted into a tight knot. "I'm getting an ulcer just thinking about it."

"Have you picked out a name?" Abigail asked.

"We're leaning toward Noelle," Brenna answered. She rubbed her lower back before asking, "What time is it now, Dylan?"

He laughed. "It's five minutes later than the last

time you asked. Why? Do you have somewhere you need to be?''

Brenna nodded and the grin on her beautiful face made Dylan feel as if he'd been punched in the gut. ''The hospital.''

''Are you sure?'' he asked, feeling as if his knees might not support him.

''Yes, darling,'' Brenna said calmly. ''I've been in labor for the last two hours.''

''Hot damn! Get the car, Pete,'' Abigail said happily. ''Looks like we might have some excitement tonight after all.''

Four hours later, in the wee hours of Christmas morning, Noelle Dyanne Chandler was born and placed into her father's waiting arms. Staring down at the most beautiful baby he'd ever seen, Dylan's chest tightened and moisture filled his eyes. He'd always been a sucker for redheads, and now he had two in his life—Brenna and his new baby daughter.

''Is she all right?'' Brenna asked anxiously.

Kissing the top of his wife's head, Dylan grinned. ''She's perfect in every way. Just like her mother.''

Brenna gave him a watery smile as he laid the baby in her arms. ''It looks like we disrupted the Christmas Jamboree again this year.''

Happier than he'd ever been in his life, Dylan grinned. ''Your grandmother's already speculating on what we'll do for next year's party.''

''That figures,'' Brenna said, sounding tired. ''Are she and Pete still out in the waiting room?''

Dylan nodded. ''I think half of Tranquillity is out there with them, too.''

''Are you serious?'' she asked, obviously shocked.

"Yep." He smiled as he touched his baby daughter's soft cheek. "They all wanted to know that you were going to be all right, and to welcome the town's newest resident." Dylan chuckled. "They were in such a hurry to get here that Cornelia, Emily and Helen wouldn't even give Myron, Ed and Luke time to change clothes. They're still dressed like Santa and his elves."

"I can't believe they all came to the hospital to wait," Brenna said, laughing.

"Darlin', don't you know what you mean to all of them?" Dylan asked, brushing a strand of copper hair from her porcelain cheek. "They love you almost as much as I do."

He watched tears fill her pretty blue eyes. "I love you, Dylan."

"And I love you, Brenna," Dylan said, leaning down to place a tender kiss on her sweet lips. "With every breath I take, I love you."

* * * * *

presents

DYNASTIES:
THE
CONNELLYS

A brand-new miniseries about the Connellys of Chicago,
a wealthy, powerful American family tied by blood to the
royal family of the island kingdom of Altaria.
They're wealthy, powerful and rocked by
scandal, betrayal…and passion!

Look for a whole year of glamorous and
utterly romantic tales in 2002:

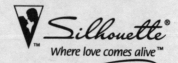

Where love comes alive™

Visit Silhouette at www.eHarlequin.com

SDDYN02

October 2002
TAMING THE OUTLAW
#1465 by Cindy Gerard

Don't miss bestselling author
Cindy Gerard's exciting story about
a sexy cowboy's reunion with his
old flame—and the daughter he
didn't know he had!

November 2002
ALL IN THE GAME
#1471 by Barbara Boswell

In the latest tale by beloved
Desire author Barbara Boswell,
a feisty beauty joins her twin as a
reality game show contestant in an
island paradise…and comes face-to-
face with her teenage crush!

December 2002
A COWBOY & A GENTLEMAN
#1477 by Ann Major

Sparks fly when two fiery Texans are
brought together by matchmaking
relatives, in this dynamic story by
the ever-popular Ann Major.

MAN OF THE MONTH

Some men are made for lovin'—and you're sure to love
these three upcoming men of the month!

Available at your favorite retail outlet.

Where love comes alive™

Visit Silhouette at www.eHarlequin.com   SDMOM02Q4

**Where royalty and romance
go hand in hand...**

The series finishes in

with these unforgettable love stories:

THE ROYAL TREATMENT
by Maureen Child
October 2002 (SD #1468)

TAMING THE PRINCE
by Elizabeth Bevarly
November 2002 (SD #1474)

ROYALLY PREGNANT
by Barbara McCauley
December 2002 (SD #1480)

Available at your favorite retail outlet.

Where love comes alive™

Jonas Thorne—
powerful, autocratic and impossible to resist.

Readers demanded more of him—
and national bestselling author
Joan Hohl granted the request!

Here in one package for the first time are
THORNE'S WAY and THORNE'S WIFE—
stories guaranteed to set your pulse racing
and heart pounding!

National Bestselling Author

JOAN HOHL

Jonas Thorne's story—in one volume

More Than Anything

Coming in December 2002.

Available only from Silhouette Books
at your favorite retail outlet.

Silhouette®
Where love comes alive™

Visit Silhouette at www.eHarlequin.com   PSMTA

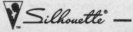
SINTMAG

Silhouette® Desire

**Meet three sexy-as-all-get-out cowboys
in Sara Orwig's new Texas crossline miniseries**

STALLION PASS

These rugged bachelors may have given up on
love...but love hasn't given up on them!

Don't miss this steamy roundup of Texan tales!

DO YOU TAKE THIS ENEMY?
November 2002 (SD #1476)

ONE TOUGH COWBOY
December 2002 (IM #1192)

THE RANCHER, THE BABY & THE NANNY
January 2003 (SD #1486)

Available at your favorite retail outlet.

Silhouette®
Where love comes alive™

COMING NEXT MONTH

#1477 A COWBOY & A GENTLEMAN—Ann Major
Zoe Duke ran off to Greece to nurse her broken heart, and the last person she expected to come face-to-face with was her high school sweetheart—the irresistible Anthony. He had made love to and then betrayed her eight years before. But he was back, and though he still made her feverish with desire, could she trust him?

#1478 CHEROKEE MARRIAGE DARE—Sheri WhiteFeather
Dynasties: The Connellys
Never one to resist a challenge, feisty Maggie Connelly vowed to save tall, dark and brooding Luke Starwind's soul. In exchange, he had to promise to marry her—if she could rescue him from his demons. Maggie ached for Luke, and while he seemed determined to keep his distance from her, *she* was determined to break him down—one kiss at a time….

#1479 A YOUNGER MAN—Rochelle Alers
Veronica Johnson-Hamlin had escaped to her vacation home for some much-needed rest and relaxation. When her car got a flat tire, J. Kumi Walker, a gorgeous ex-marine ten years her junior, came to her aid. Veronica quickly discovered how much she and Kumi had in common—including a sizzling attraction. But would family problems and their age difference keep them apart?

#1480 ROYALLY PREGNANT—Barbara McCauley
Crown and Glory
Forced to do the bidding of terrorists in exchange for her grandmother's life, Emily Bridgewater staged an accident, faked amnesia and set out to seduce Prince Dylan Penwyck. But Emily hadn't counted on falling for her handsome target. Dylan was everything she wanted…and the father of her unborn child. She only hoped he would forgive her once he learned the truth.

#1481 HER TEXAN TEMPTATION—Shirley Rogers
Upon her father's death, Mary Beth Adams returned to Texas to take over her family's ranch. She would do anything to keep the ranch—even accept help from cowboy Deke McCall, the man she'd always secretly loved. There was an undeniable attraction between them, but Mary Beth wanted more than just Deke's body—she wanted his heart!

#1482 BABY & THE BEAST—Laura Wright
When millionaire recluse Michael Wulf rescued a very pregnant Isabella Spencer from a blizzard, he didn't expect to have to deliver her baby, Emily. Days passed, and Michael's frozen heart began to thaw in response to lovely Isabella's hot kisses. Michael yearned to be a part of Isabella's life, but could he let go of the past and embrace the love of a lifetime?

SDCNM1102